Missouri
State Facts

Nickname:	Show-Me State
Date Entered Union:	August 10, 1821 (the 24th state)
Motto:	*Salus populi suprema lex esto* (The welfare of the people shall be the supreme law)
Missouri Men:	Robert Altman, *film director* Burt Bacharach, *songwriter* Yogi Berra, *baseball player* Samuel Langhorne Clemens (Mark Twain), *author* Walter Cronkite, *TV newscaster*
Tree:	American dogwood
Name's Origin:	Named after Missouri Indian tribe whose name means "town of the large canoes."
Fun Fact:	At the St. Louis World's Fair in 1904, the ice cream cone was invented.

He stirred restlessly on the sofa, his thoughts still on the woman upstairs.

Those eyes, those beautiful sapphire eyes. A man could melt into those blue depths, or he could be pulled up short by the strength and determination that lingered there. Most women would have completely fallen apart under these dangerous circumstances, yet Libby had remained firmly in control. There was more to the lady than met the eye, and this somehow pleased Tony.

He leaned back and closed his eyes, remembering that instant in her apartment when he'd pulled her tightly against him. The blue teddy did little to hide her rounded curves and slender hips, the silky length of her long legs. He'd been shocked at the unexpected flare of desire that ripped through him, a desire that was becoming impossible to resist....

American

HEROES

AGAINST ALL ODDS

One of the
Good Guys

Carla
CASSIDY

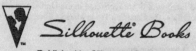

Silhouette Books

Published by Silhouette Books
America's Publisher of Contemporary Romance

SILHOUETTE BOOKS
300 East 42nd St.,
New York, N.Y. 10017

ISBN 0-373-82223-5

ONE OF THE GOOD GUYS

Copyright © 1993 by Carla Bracale

Visit Silhouette at www.eHarlequin.com

Printed in U.S.A.

About the Author

Award-winning author **Carla Cassidy** has written over thirty-five books for Silhouette. In 1995 she won Best Silhouette Romance from *Romantic Times Magazine* for *Anything for Danny*. In 1998 she also won a Career Achievement Award for Best Innovative Series from *Romantic Times Magazine*.

Carla believes the only thing better than curling up with a good book to read is sitting down at the computer with a good story to write. She's looking forward to writing many more books and bringing hours of pleasure to readers.

Dear Reader,

Tony Pandolinni sprang to life fully formed in my mind long before I actually started to write *One of the Good Guys*. With dark curly hair, intense eyes and a dark mustache to add to his slightly dangerous, devastating attractiveness, I felt as if I knew this man intimately...or at least wanted to!

It seemed only right that he should be a private eye, one of those good guys with a little bit of attitude hiding an enormous, vulnerable heart. Of course, I had to give him just the right kind of woman. I made sure heroine Libby Weatherby, smart and sassy, was more than a challenge for the sexy Tony.

Funny, when Tony first came to mind, I felt as if I knew him. To tell the truth, I married him. Tony looks just like my husband, and I think he's one sexy good guy!

I hope you enjoy reading Tony and Libby's story as much as I enjoyed writing it. Happy reading!

Carla Cassidy

Please address questions and book requests to:
Silhouette Reader Service
U.S.: 3010 Walden Ave., P.O. Box 1325, Buffalo, NY 14269
Canadian: P.O. Box 609, Fort Erie, Ont. L2A 5X3

Chapter 1

She was being followed again. Libby had suspected it only minutes after locking the door of the pawnshop and climbing into her car. Now that she thought about it, she realized it was the same car that had been everywhere she had been for the past three days. As she watched in the rearview mirror, the tan Buick kept a steady, even distance from her.

Had this been the first time, she might have panicked, wondering why she was being tailed and by whom. But it was not the first time. In fact, she'd lost count of the number of times her footsteps had been echoed, her movements shadowed, her life observed. Now, after almost three months of being under constant surveillance, she was tired of the game.

"Enough is enough," she muttered, stepping down on the gas pedal, effortlessly maneuvering her sports car in and out of traffic. She had become quite proficient at losing inept private investigators, and if this one was as inefficient as the last two had been, she should have no problems giving him the slip in the evening rush-hour traffic.

Logically, she knew Bill would have provided the investigator with the necessary information—name, address, employment and regular habits. She also knew that eventually her pursuer would catch up to her, but it gave her a perverse satisfaction to speed along, zigzagging across lanes and between other cars, imagining the panic on her pursuer's face as she left him farther and farther behind.

"Eat my dust," she murmured with a grin, watching in her mirror as the Buick disappeared in the heavy flow of traffic behind her.

After several more minutes of evasive driving, certain that she had lost him, she slowed down and took a deep, steadying breath. Her playful mood of moments before had changed into a burning, seething resentment.

"Damn him," she expelled, hitting the steering wheel with the palm of her hand. It was not the man in the Buick she cursed. He was merely a paid employee. Her curse instead was directed at the man who had been her husband for three long years, the man who had been her ex-husband for the past eight months. Why couldn't Bill just face the fact that their marriage was over, dead?

Libby rolled down the window, enjoying the gusty early spring wind that whipped her pale hair around her head. Her thoughts lingered on her ex-husband. Poor Bill—even in her anger, she could almost feel sympathetic for the macho, overprotective, smothering construction worker she'd married, then divorced as a means of self-preservation.

She'd tried to make the marriage work. For three long years she had put her wants and needs aside to accommodate Bill's. She'd stayed home and waited patiently for his return when he went out on his weekly drinking binges with his construction buddies. She'd even managed to convince herself that he didn't occasionally come home reeking of another woman's cheap perfume.

The end of the marriage had come abruptly. She'd awakened one morning wanting to scream from the strain of trying to be something she was not.

Instead of screaming, she filed for a divorce. She'd tried to be kind, tried to convince Bill that he'd be much happier with a different woman. But it was as if the divorce suddenly spurred a case of undying love in Bill. Unfortunately, his efforts to revive the marriage had been a case of too little too late.

Bill was certain the divorce was caused by another man. He'd hired the investigators to prove the fact and to somehow remain linked to her life.

But there was no other man. In the past eight months, the most exciting thing the investigators could have reported was that Libby's cat, Twilight, had developed a hair ball and had to be rushed to the vet's office.

A small smile curved her lips as she thought of the private eye she'd just left behind. At least he had been a little better than the rest. It *had* been three days before that she'd initially noticed him behind her. Three days, she mused. She'd caught on to the previous investigators immediately. A giggle escaped her as she remembered a month ago, when an overzealous investigator had accidently bumped into the rear of her car in his zest to stay on her tail. The giggle blossomed into a snort of laughter as she thought of the hot blush that had reddened the man's chubby, florid face as she told him to give her regards to Bill.

The smile that lit her face now died abruptly as she

turned down the street where her apartment building was. Her gaze landed on the tan Buick already parked in her usual parking space.

How on earth had he managed that? She had driven the most direct route home and was certain he hadn't passed her. A small hint of respect at his finesse grudgingly arose inside her. The man was good. The man was definitely good.

As she slowly drove past the car, she turned and scrutinized the occupant, giving him her total, undivided attention.

Shock pierced through her as she stared at him. He wasn't a dumpy, florid-faced, thick-necked investigator. Oh, no. His features were sharply defined in the golden light of dusk. Dark curls, just this side of unruly, topped his head. A wide forehead gave way to dark, intense eyes and a straight, arrogant nose. A full, dark mustache hid his upper lip and as their gazes met, he gestured as if tipping an imaginary hat to her, showing her a flash of the glittering whiteness of perfect teeth as he smiled in obvious amusement.

His smile effectively broke the trancelike spell she had momentarily fallen into, and she gunned the motor and roared by him, shooting into a parking space halfway down the block. Once there, she remained in the car, mentally steadying herself from the shock of his unexpected attractiveness.

He possessed a handsomeness that hinted at danger. Physically speaking, he was the type who could either play the hero, saving the heroine from the clutches of death, or the villain—dangerously handsome, luring the hapless, innocent heroine into trouble.

She shook her head, effectively dispelling the fanciful thoughts. She was allowing her imagination to run wild.

Still, she knew instinctively she'd rather have this man on her side than have to face him as an adversary.

She shut off the engine and fumbled with the key ring until she held her apartment key firmly in hand. She got out of her car and walked hurriedly toward the brick building, her slender shoulders militarily straight. She was self-conscious that a dark, glittering gaze followed her every movement.

At the front door of the building she paused impulsively. With an impish grin, she turned and waved two fingers at the handsome investigator, then turned and entered the apartment building.

Once inside her fourth-floor apartment, she flipped on all the lights against the darkening night and kicked off her high-heeled shoes. Flopping down on the couch, she smiled as the gray tomcat greeted her by jumping up and sitting on her chest. "Hi, Twilight," she murmured, scratching the cat affectionately behind his furry ears. "Did you miss me today?"

The cat meowed plaintively, then jumped down on the floor and looked at her expectantly.

"Okay, okay." Rising off the sofa, she went into the small kitchen, the cat a shadow at her heels. She grabbed a can of cat food that, according to Twilight, tasted better than it smelled. With efficiency born of habit, she opened the can and dumped the contents into the dish on the floor. "There you go," she muttered maternally, once again petting the tomcat's soft fur as he lapped greedily at the fishy-smelling food.

She went back into the living room, drawn to the window that provided a perfect view to the street below. She pulled the curtain aside a fraction of an inch, just enough to peer out and see that the Buick was still parked below. She jerked the curtain closed as the phone rang shrilly. Flopping down on the sofa once again, she picked up the receiver.

"How's my favorite girl?" a deep voice asked without preamble.

"Vinnie!" Libby smiled at the sound of her father's familiar voice. "How is life in sunny Florida?"

"Hot, humid and full of husband-hungry widows," he answered with a snort. "I love it," he added with a gusty explosion of laughter. "How are things there?"

"About the same as usual. The shop keeps me busy. You know business is always good in the spring when people clean out their attics and basements."

"Are you still dragging home abandoned crap?"

Libby laughed. "Anything that's left unclaimed, and you know it isn't crap. It's history. Everything I bring home talks to me."

"Huh, some men my age get grandchildren. I get a daughter whose furniture talks to her." His gruff voice was full of affection. "What do you hear from that ex-husband of yours? Has he finally decided to leave you alone?"

"No such luck. As a matter of fact, there is a new detective sitting outside my apartment at this very moment." Libby sighed. "Bill called me the other night wanting a reconciliation. He sounded like he'd had too much to drink. I think he figures I'll get tired of being spied on and go back to him."

"Will you?"

"Not a chance," Libby answered without hesitation.

"You know all I want is for you to be happy. Well, I just wanted to check and see how you were getting along." Vinnie began winding down the conversation and Libby smiled at the mental picture she had of him checking his watch and mentally calculating the cost of the long-distance phone call.

"I love you, Vinnie," she breathed softly into the phone.

"I love you, too, doll. I'll call you the same time next week." With that he clicked off.

Libby replaced the receiver slowly, thoughtfully. She was glad her father was happy in Florida, but there were times when she really missed him. Since her mother's death when she was three years old, it had always been Vinnie and Libby.

"Did you finish your gourmet supper?" she asked the cat, who strode regally across the floor from the kitchen and stretched out languidly on a colorful hook rug, his contented purring instantly filling the silence of the room.

Yawning, Libby stretched and looked at the antique clock that sat on the walnut bric-a-brac shelf. It was only a few minutes after eight o'clock, but she was exhausted. It had been a particularly busy day at the pawnshop.

She got up from the sofa with another tired yawn and went into the bedroom. She walked over to the wardrobe in the corner and pulled out a blue lace teddy. Laying it on the bed, she quickly undressed, pulling off the skirt and blouse she had worn to work that day. Slip and hose quickly followed, landing in a heap in the middle of the floor. She stepped into the teddy and pulled it up, pausing as her hand encountered the heavy gold necklace resting around her neck.

Going into the bathroom, she turned the necklace around and peered into the mirror above the sink, fumbling for a few moments with the sturdy, complicated fastening. Finally the necklace unclasped, sliding down her throat. She caught it and carried it into her bedroom where she set it on the table next to the bed.

It was a beautiful piece. It had been brought in only that morning by a diminutive old man. Libby had tried to talk him into pawning it, but he had insisted he wanted to sell it outright. He'd seemed anxious, in a hurry, and had accepted her first offer.

She turned down the blankets on her bed, a smile curving her lips as she thought of her conversation with Vinnie. Like the necklace, most of her apartment furnishings were items from the pawnshop, things that had never been reclaimed or items she'd bought outright. She tried to tell herself she brought them home for safekeeping, but the truth was she loved the curious mishmash of things people brought in to sell or to pawn for extra money.

On impulse, she walked back into the living room and shut off all the lights. She drew open her curtains and looked down on the street below. Still there... He was still down there watching her, spying on her. Her eyes narrowed as she saw the glow of a cigarette arcing away from the car window.

Good, let him stay down there all night, smoke a hundred cigarettes and develop a bad case of smoker's cough. Maybe it would be cold tonight and he would be miserable in the confines of his car. Or better yet, let it rain...an arctic downpour that would chill him to the bones.

She turned away from the window with a smug smile of satisfaction, content that she had wished all the bad things she could think of on him. After all, it served him right. If he was going to intrude on her privacy, the least she could do was curse him to a horrible fate. She stifled a yawn with the back of her hand, allowing the curtains to fall back into place, then went back into the bedroom.

She crawled into bed and shut off the bedside lamp and within seconds she felt the bed depress beneath the weight of Twilight. Within minutes, Libby slept.

In the street below, Tony Pandolinni watched the light of the fourth-floor apartment go out. He slowly climbed out of the Buick and stretched his long, lean legs, almost enjoying the sensation of needles and pins that tickled at his feet, signaling that circulation had begun once again.

In all the advice, all the opinions he had solicited before leaving the police department and starting his own detective agency, nobody had mentioned the fact that the greatest risk a private detective faced was the loss of a limb from lack of circulation and/or death from perpetual boredom.

In the past year since beginning his own business, he had suffered plenty of both. While this particular assignment was proving quite boring, at least the subject was pleasant to look at. In fact, she was more than just pleasant—she was really very pretty.

His lips curved into a soft smile as he thought of the way she had waved her fingers at him just before disappearing into her apartment building. She had wanted him to know that she was on to him, that she was aware of the fact that he was following her. Her action had shown a certain amount of spunk. No wonder her ex-husband was reluctant to cut his ties with her. Pretty and spunky—it was an appealing package...

Tony shoved these thoughts from his mind. Keeping an eye on Libby Weatherby was merely a job. He'd give this particular job one more night and day, then he'd report back to the husband that Libby lived a boring, solitary existence. Then that would be the end of that.

He leaned back against his car and shook a cigarette out of the pack. Another hazard of this line of work—one tended to smoke too much. A nasty habit…he'd been trying unsuccessfully to quit for months. He lit the cigarette, his gaze going back to the darkened fourth-floor window. It was going to be a long, boring night.

Libby awoke suddenly, aware of some sort of activity taking place at the foot of the bed. She opened her eyes to see Twilight contentedly gnawing on the toe of her last pair of good panty hose.

"Twilight!" She sat up and swatted at the cat, then moaned as she picked up the tattered remains of the hose. "Dumb cat," she muttered sleepily, sliding from the bed and heading for the bathroom.

Twenty minutes later she emerged freshly showered and clad in a beige lacy bra and matching panties. She stood in front of the open wardrobe, indecisively staring at the clothes before her. It was so difficult to dress for spring in the Midwest, where the temperature could fluctuate as much as thirty degrees in a single day. She finally settled on a pair of jeans and a lightweight, crew-neck sweater. She added the heavy gold necklace and a pair of earrings. As she applied her makeup, she cast a scurrilous gaze at the errant cat who had returned to his position at the foot of the bed, resuming his task of totally shredding the panty hose.

Then, ready to face a new day, Libby left the apartment. She studiously ignored the Buick and its driver, who was still in the same position as the night before. She continued to ignore his vigilance as she headed her car toward the pawnshop, vowing that tonight she would have it out with Bill. Tonight she would tell him to call off his bloodhounds or else he'd be slapped with some sort of harassment charge. They were legally divorced. She'd tried to be nice, she'd tried to maintain a friendship, but now it was time to cut the umbilical cord.

This issue settled in her mind, she turned on the radio, enjoying the rhythmic mellow rock music that immediately filled the car. The upbeat melody caused an uplifting optimism to course through her veins. It was a beautiful morning, and she was looking forward to what this day in the shop would bring. That was one good thing about owning a pawnshop—no two days were ever the same.

She parked her car in front of the store, in the space reserved for her. A feeling of pride swelled in her heart as she stepped up to the front door, her gaze lingering on the bold black lettering that proclaimed Vinnie's Pawnshop. When her father had retired almost a year before, she had never considered changing the name. For twenty-five years it had been Vinnie's, and it was going to remain that way. With a smile, she unlocked the door and walked in.

For a moment her mind refused to assess what lay before her. The entire contents of the shop lay topsy-turvy. Knickknacks and dishes had been smashed and shards of glass littered the floor, crunching and snapping beneath Libby's tentative footsteps.

Furniture had been tossed helter-skelter, with no respect for age or value. As if in a dream—no, some horrible nightmare—she walked slowly toward the small office door at the back of the shop, cringing at the senseless vandalism that surrounded her.

The scene in her office was worse. Her desk drawers had been emptied and papers were strewn all over the floor. The entire place looked as if a miniature but destructive tornado had swept full force through the store.

My God... Her mind reeled with shock as she leaned weakly against the wooden desk. What had happened here? And why? As shock began to wear off, anger took its place.

The police...she needed the police. They would find out who did this. They would punish the person who had destroyed her shop.

Angry tears blinded Libby as she ran back out into the bright sunshine, seeking the reassuring blue uniform of a police officer. Her tears came faster and faster as she stood helplessly in the center of the sidewalk, unsure where to go for help.

She screamed as a hand suddenly came down firmly on her slender shoulders.

Chapter 2

Libby gasped, stifling another scream and jerking away in fear from the hands that touched her. She whirled around and stared up at the man who had been following her for the past few days. The terror in her eyes quickly died, replaced with a seething, uncontrollable anger.

"You!" She glared at him with burning, reproachful eyes. "Did you and Bill have something to do with this?" She gestured wildly at the shop. "Is this some sort of scam to prove that I can't survive on my own? Well, it won't work. You can just go back and tell Bill that his little scheme is stupid. Nothing and nobody can make me go back to him."

Without saying a word, the man walked over to the shop and opened the door. His brow wrinkled and his jaw muscles tightened as with one quick glance he assessed the situation. "I would suggest a call to the police would be in order."

"Thank you, Mr. Sherlock Holmes," she snapped sarcastically, her shoulders sagging as her anger vanished, usurped by an overwhelming sense of despair. She blinked rapidly to dispel the hot tears that were once again threatening to fall.

He placed a hand on her shoulder, this time not firmly but softly, as if in sympathy. "Is there a phone in your shop?" His voice was a pleasant, low-pitched rumble.

She nodded, biting her bottom lip and allowing him to lead her back into the shop. Once inside, she stood in the center of the rubble, vaguely aware that the man was talking on the telephone.

As he murmured softly into the receiver, giving all the pertinent information, Libby looked around, assessing the damage. She moved to straighten a lamp shade on a brass lamp, then picked up a wooden chair that was lying on its side.

"You really shouldn't touch anything until the police arrive."

She turned at the sound of his deep voice, realizing he had hung up the phone and now stood looking at her.

"Why don't you look around and see if you can discover if anything has been stolen," he suggested.

She nodded, relieved to be able to do something—anything. Her fingers itched with the need to straighten and clean, but she realized that his advice about not touching anything until the police arrived was sensible.

She walked around the small confines of the shop, her gaze darting from place to place. She was slightly perturbed by the fact that she was drawn again and again to the handsome man who was now casually leaning against the inner-office door, his eyes darkly inscrutable.

She couldn't help but notice that he was a magnificent specimen of masculinity. The night before, she had only gotten a view of him from the neck up. Now she was unsurprised and somehow pleased to discover that his body perfectly suited his head. He was sleekly toned, dangerously fit, and clad in a shirt that accentuated his broad shoulders and slender waistline. His blue jeans were tight, hugging and molding his lean hips and muscular legs. He did not have the physique of a man who worked out with weights, but was lean and wiry, possessing the physical attributes one usually ascribed to a swimmer or a runner.

There was little physical evidence that he had spent the entire night in the cramped confines of a car. His shirt was slightly rumpled and his lower face had a dark shadow that attested to a morning without shaving. Other than that, he looked as fresh and vital as if he'd spent the night in his own comfortable bed.

She pulled her gaze away with an audible sigh of irritation. What the hell was she doing, admiring the physical attributes of a virtual stranger while her livelihood lay in shambles around her?

"Anything missing?"

She shook her head slowly. "Nothing that I can tell right offhand." She sat down on the wooden chair she had righted moments before, once again looking at him. "I'm sorry…about what I said earlier. I was upset. I know Bill had nothing to do with this. Even *he* wouldn't stoop this low."

He merely nodded, his expression unreadable.

"I'm sure you know my name…but I…uh…don't know yours." She stifled a nervous giggle. God, her shop had been broken into, ransacked and vandalized, and she was sitting here, casually asking the name of a man who had been hired to follow her every move for the past three days. Could things get any more ludicrous?

He smiled, flashing beautiful, white teeth. "I'm Tony Pandolinni."

At that moment two patrol cars pulled to a halt outside the shop, their sirens whooping the news that something was amiss.

The next two hours passed quickly as the officers surveyed the damage, discovered where a crowbar had been used to break the lock of the back door and asked questions, questions and more questions.

Libby was totally wrung out by the endless interrogation of the police officers. No, there had been no guns kept on the premises. It was a personal managerial position to never accept firearms. No, she hadn't been aware of any recent customers who had been angry or upset enough to commit this senseless vandalism.

The officers, with Libby's help, discovered that the only thing that appeared to be missing was Libby's daily ledger, a diary of sorts with each day's transactions written up in detail. The stereos, VCR equipment, televisions—even the cash in the register—remained intact and untouched.

The officers dutifully wrote everything down in small black notebooks, then left, but not before voicing their own personal opinions that the break-in had probably been committed by kids out for an evening of destruction.

After the police left, Libby immediately began straightening the clutter, wondering if the shop would ever be the same.

"Maybe you should just leave this mess for today. Go home and relax," Tony suggested.

She jumped in surprise at the sound of his voice, having forgotten his presence in the store. She shook her head. "I could never rest knowing this mess was here."

He nodded as if in understanding, and to her surprise he picked up a broom that had been standing in a corner. He began sweeping up the slivers of broken glass that glistened in the sunlight pouring through the large front window of the shop.

"You don't have to do that," she protested.

"I know, I want to." He flashed her that devastating grin, then resumed his sweeping.

Libby watched him for a moment longer, then shrugged and went back to work. At her request, Tony kept the sightseers out of the shop, allowing in only the regular customers whom Libby first okayed.

It was almost another two hours later when Libby sat down tiredly on a chair and looked around her, grateful to see that the shop had been put back into some semblance of order. She sighed, then jerked upward in the chair as a loud banging noise came from the back rooms. Noting that Tony had disappeared, she followed the sound to discover him boarding up the back door.

She watched him silently for a moment, almost able to see the taut muscles of his back flexing and working through the fabric of his shirt as he applied hammer to nails. He finished driving in the last nail, then turned to her and smiled. "Hope you don't mind. I found the hammer and nails back here and thought I'd put them to good use. This should hold until a new door can be properly installed."

She nodded her thanks, then walked back to the front of the store, where she flopped tiredly into a chair and pushed her damp, blond hair away from her face with the back of her hand.

He sat down on a chair across the room and looked

around. "I'd say we did a good day's work, Libby Weatherby."

"And I thank you for all your help," she said simply.

He nodded, then stood up and walked over to stand before her. He knelt in front of her and pulled a pristine handkerchief from his back pocket. In a quick, gentle motion he wiped the cloth across her forehead.

"What...what was that for?" she asked, jerking back from his momentary contact.

He smiled, making her notice the fine webbing of wrinkles that radiated out from his dark eyes. "I never take a woman to lunch who has dirt streaked across her forehead."

"And what makes you think I'm going to have lunch with you?" she asked peevishly, suddenly very hot and tired.

"It's after noon. I'm hungry and I imagine you are, too. You've had a harrowing day. Surely you can close up shop early after such an experience."

She started to protest, irritated at his presumption that she would have lunch with him. Still, he was right. She was rather hungry and she really wasn't in the mood to keep the store open for the rest of the afternoon. She was exhausted and bewildered, and at the moment nothing sounded more appealing than a restaurant meal before going home to a warm shower and a long nap.

"I am hungry," she admitted aloud.

"There's a little café on the next block. It's supposed to have great food. Olive's—have you ever eaten there?"

"Many times. I often go there for lunch." Decision made, Libby stood up and grabbed her purse. "Okay," she agreed.

At the door of the shop she paused, her gaze lingering

on the contents, basically back in order, but not quite the same as before.

"Anything wrong?" he asked, stepping out onto the sidewalk.

She shook her head slowly, then pulled the door closed and carefully locked it. How could she explain to him that somehow the shop now seemed tainted, blemished? A stranger, or several strangers, had wandered around, touching things, breaking things, effectively destroying the peace she'd always felt while in the store.

They walked in silence toward the café, and Libby's thoughts turned to the man beside her. What kind of person was he? How could he make his living by following people, spying on people? She'd always thought those kind of paid voyeurs were sleazy, but Tony Pandolinni didn't appear to be a sleaze bag. He was not only attractive to a fault, he'd also been kind enough to help her with the cleanup.

Maybe over lunch she could ask him to appeal to Bill, to get him to stop this senseless, constant surveillance. If that could be accomplished from this mess, then maybe it would all be worthwhile. It would be nice to be able to call her life her own again, to no longer feel the presence of someone constantly watching her, following her.

They entered Olive's Café and sat down at a booth toward the back of the small restaurant.

"Hi, Libby." Olive waddled to their booth, barely able to fit her massive bulk between the tables. "I hear there was some excitement over at your place this morning."

"Hmm, a break-in and a big mess, but nothing of value was stolen," Libby replied, noticing the way Olive looked at Tony hungrily, as if he were a thick, juicy red steak.

"What can I get for you folks today?" Olive's gaze never wavered from Tony, and to Libby's utter disgust, Tony actually winked at the big woman.

"I'd like a hamburger, fries and a glass of ice tea." Libby snapped her menu shut, already regretting the impulse that had led her to agree to have lunch with the virtual stranger across from her. Her day had been horrendous enough, and the last thing she needed was to spend time with a mini-Magnum who'd probably skated through life on the magnetic attraction of his high cheekbones and dimpled chin.

"And what about you?" Olive grinned broadly at Tony, then leaned toward him with a conspiratorial whisper. "I have it on good authority that the spaghetti sauce is exceptional today."

"Homemade?" Tony raised a dark eyebrow.

"By these very own hands," Olive said with an uncharacteristic girlish giggle.

"That's good enough for me." Tony grinned at her, handing her his menu, his body leaned toward her attentively.

"And for you, I put a couple of extra meatballs on the plate."

"Ah, you're a real charmer." Tony gave the broad woman the benefit of his hundred-watt smile.

Libby watched this byplay with disgust, unable to believe that even a hardened, world-wise woman like Olive could be affected by male physical attractiveness. "I've been eating in this restaurant almost every day for the past several months, and never has Olive offered to put something extra on my plate," she commented, picking up her paper napkin and positioning it on her lap.

Tony shrugged and looked at her innocently. "Perhaps you just don't know how to order properly."

"Or flirt outrageously," Libby muttered beneath her breath.

For a moment he merely stared at her; then he grinned slowly. "Ah, is it possible the beautiful flower perhaps has thorns?" He reached across the table and lightly touched one of her hands.

"It is very possible, and it's dangerous to get too close to a thorny flower. You're liable to get stuck." She withdrew her hand and moved it out of his reach, irritated by the sudden infusion of warmth that had coursed through her at his light touch.

"There are some men who thrive on danger." He grinned easily, seemingly unaffected by her withdrawal from him. "Is that why you and your husband divorced? Because you're full of thorns?"

"Is that why you decided to become a private investigator? Because you thrive on danger?" Libby countered coolly.

Once again Tony's gaze was thoughtful as another small grin played on his lips, making his mustache twitch beguilingly. "Very good—when the conversation gets too personal, it's always a good tactic to counter with a question." He shrugged in good-natured defeat. "Okay, we'll talk about me. I'm thirty-six years old. I was a police officer for eleven years. I was a damn good cop, but I decided I was ready to go into business for myself. I've been a private investigator for almost a year now."

"Business must be pretty bad if you have to take cases like Bill's," Libby exclaimed with a touch of sourness, not forgetting for a moment that this man had been shadowing her life for the past three days.

Tony shrugged. "Actually, I usually don't take these kind of cases…but to be perfectly honest, this particular surveillance case intrigued me."

"Intrigued you?" Libby gave a short burst of unbelieving laughter. "What could you possibly find intriguing about Bill and me?"

"Oh, it wasn't so much Bill. He just appeared to me to be a lovesick, obsessed ex-husband. What intrigued me the most was that he told me he'd hired two prior detectives and you'd caught on to all of them within hours."

Libby nodded, wry humor lifting her features as she thought of the previous P.I.s' ineptitude. "I'll admit, you were much better than the others. You've been following me for three days. All the others lasted only a single day."

His dark eyes glinted with suppressed amusement, and a small smile touched his lips. "Actually, I've been following you for six days." He laughed at her expression of shock, his laughter deep and pleasant. "You're good, but I'm better."

"I don't believe you," she said flatly, looking at him skeptically. Her mind whirled back over the past six days. Surely she would have known if somebody had been following her for almost an entire week. "I…I would have sensed you…I would have known…"

He reached into his shirt pocket and withdrew a small black notebook. Thumbing through the pages, he came to a halt and began reading aloud. "Wednesday evening, subject stopped for groceries on way home from work, then proceeded directly to her apartment. Subject went to bed at ten o'clock." He looked up from the notebook, the teasing laughter back in his eyes. "Oh, by the way,

I find that little blue thing you wear to bed quite attractive."

She opened and closed her mouth several times, sputtering in total outrage. For a moment her indignation was so great, words wouldn't come, and so she settled for glaring at him. "That is absolutely despicable," she finally managed to sputter, grabbing her purse, intent on leaving. She was stymied by Olive, whose massive bulk appeared at their table with their orders, effectively blocking Libby's desired escape.

Once the big woman had departed from their table, Libby glared at him once again. "I think you're rude and obnoxious, and I think the job you perform is equally odious." She fumed silently for a moment, then turned her attention to the hamburger before her, wanting only to eat, then go home and leave behind this man who'd invaded her privacy so completely. Imagine... he'd actually seen her in her teddy. Her face shook as she guided a hot French fry toward her mouth.

"I'm sorry if I upset you," Tony offered, but Libby didn't think he sounded the least bit sorry. In fact, he sounded quite amused, and this only served to infuriate her further.

She retreated into a silence that grew as both of them concentrated on their lunch.

"A pawnshop is rather an unusual business for a young woman, isn't it?" He broke the uncomfortable silence.

"What's wrong with a woman being a pawnbroker?" she asked defensively.

"Nothing. I just said it was unusual. Are you always so touchy?"

"Only with snakes who've been spying on me," she snapped, refusing to look at him.

"Libby." His voice softly cajoled.

She looked up to see him waving his white napkin, which he'd stuck on the prongs of his fork. "Can't we call a truce, at least for the remainder of the meal? Hostility always gives me indigestion."

In spite of her anger, Libby felt herself soften a touch. He looked so ridiculous, waving the makeshift flag in front of his handsome face. "All right, a truce. But just for the remainder of the meal." She smiled slowly. "I wouldn't want to be responsible for anyone's discomfort due to indigestion."

"Good. Now tell me how you came to be in the pawnshop business." He replaced the napkin in his lap and smiled at her expectantly.

"I practically grew up in the pawnshop. It never entered my mind to do anything else." Her features softened and a smile touched her lips, her earlier anger tempered by thoughts of Vinnie. "My father always told me I was brought into the pawnshop by an angel who pawned me in exchange for a harp of gold." She laughed softly. "For the longest time I couldn't figure it out because I always thought gold harps were standard equipment that every angel received upon entering heaven. You know, every angel got wings, a white robe and a harp of gold."

"Your father sounds like a very special man," Tony observed.

"Oh, he is. My mother died when I was very young. My father raised me. He's a tough old cougar, very strong and independent."

"And I have a feeling his daughter has an independent streak in her, as well," Tony said, efficiently twirling a bite of spaghetti neatly onto his fork and popping it into his mouth.

"Something my ex-husband couldn't accept," Libby explained. Then, realizing she had provided herself with the opening she'd been looking for, she continued. "Speaking of Bill, I'd like you to do me a favor. When you report back to him or whatever it is you private eyes do, please tell him to stop this harassment of my life. Tell him to stop spying on me."

"He doesn't think of it as spying. From what he told me, he thinks of it more like a guardian angel service he's providing for you. He's concerned about the neighborhood where you live, the kind of work you do."

"But that's ridiculous. I don't need a guardian angel," Libby scoffed. "All I want is to be left alone to get on with my life." She pushed away her half-eaten hamburger.

"He still loves you," Tony said, as if to explain Bill's actions to her.

"He doesn't love me—he thinks he does, but he doesn't. He just doesn't like to lose. He's sure that I left him for another man, and he won't be satisfied until he's proved the fact. That absolves him from failure. Then the breakup isn't his fault, it's the 'other man's.'" She closed her mouth, realizing she'd said far too much.

They finished the meal in silence as Libby withdrew into herself, mentally contemplating the problems the vandalized shop held for her. She would have to contact her insurance company about the dishes and vases that had been destroyed. She cringed inwardly at this thought. She'd already paid an exorbitant price for insurance. Another rise in the premiums would really crimp her budget.

Still, that thought didn't begin to depress her as much as the task of telling some of her customers that their items had been destroyed. Her customers had entrusted their valuables to her, believing she would hold those items safely until a time when they could come back and claim them. She had betrayed their trust, and it was this knowledge that pained her more than anything.

"Are you all right?" Tony's eyes gazed at her sympathetically, making her aware of how sensitive he seemed to be to her moods.

She nodded. "I was just thinking about the mess at the shop—all the things that were broken. Monetarily speaking, none of the things were worth much, but to my customers many of the items were invaluable."

"You can't blame yourself for the break-in," Tony said, pushing away his now-empty plate and shaking a cigarette out of the pack.

"Yes, but I should have had some sort of security system installed...or something—" She broke off helplessly.

"You're the victim, remember? Don't make the mistake of blaming yourself. If you want to lay blame, do it at the doorstep of the person who broke into your shop, but don't blame yourself." His voice rang with an authority and conviction she couldn't ignore, and she nodded at him gratefully.

"Ready?" he asked, standing up as he lit his cigarette.

"Ready," she agreed, also rising. She fumbled in her purse and pulled out a twenty-dollar bill. "Lunch is on me," she said firmly as they approached the cashier.

"Oh, no. I invited you to lunch," Tony protested.

"Please, I want to do this. After all the help you gave me in cleaning up the shop, I feel like I owe you," she said earnestly.

"And I'll just bet you always make sure you aren't obligated to anyone for anything," he observed, a touch of amusement making his mustache twitch once again.

"Okay." He relented after a moment. "Lunch is on you. Are you going back to the shop?"

She shook her head. The morning events had been too unsettling. "No, I think I'll just go home and make some phone calls to the insurance people." She looked at him curiously. "So, what are you going to do now that your cover has been blown and you won't be following me anymore?" she asked as they left the restaurant.

"The first thing I intend to do is sleep for about twenty-four hours." He smiled and for the first time she noticed that he looked tired. "Then I'll wait for the next case to come up."

"Will you have to wait long?"

He shrugged. "As long as it takes. In the meantime, I have several ongoing jobs with large companies as a sort of unofficial security consultant. I come in periodically and check out their security systems, evaluate their effectiveness and make suggestions as to how the systems can be improved." They stopped walking as they arrived at Libby's car. "I'll follow you home," Tony said.

"That really isn't necessary," she protested stiffly, some of her earlier resentment coming back.

"But I insist. I always see my subjects home." He opened her car door, allowing her to slide in behind the steering wheel. "I'll be right behind you."

"Oh, no, you won't," Libby muttered as he slammed her car door. She started the engine and took off, laughing aloud when she caught sight of Tony's surprised expression as he realized she wasn't waiting around for him. She turned the steering wheel, pulling into the traffic and ignoring the honk of the irate driver she'd cut off as she'd pulled out.

There was no rhyme or reason to her actions—he

knew where she was going, he knew where she lived. But this little game of beating him there made her feel exceedingly good. She wanted no more investigations of her life. She simply wanted to be left alone.

She drove as fast as traffic would allow, determined to be inside her apartment before he could catch up to her. She'd be satisfied if she never saw a private eye for the remainder of her life.

She whirled the steering wheel, rounding the corner that led to her apartment and braking with a squeal of astonishment. There, in her parking space, was the tan Buick. Even from where she sat, she could see the wide grin of amusement that lit Tony's face.

She muttered an oath of irritation and pulled her car to the curb. The man was living up to the title of guardian angel, for the only way he could have beaten her here was to have flown.

"I told you...you're good, but I'm better."

She looked up to see him standing beside her car, a lazy smile on his arrogant face.

"I don't find you amusing," she retorted, making him jump aside as she threw open her car door.

"Oh, and I was trying so hard," he said lightly, then added in a more serious tone. "I told you, I always see my subjects safely home."

"But you've forgotten. I'm no longer your subject." Libby walked toward the building, her anger making her steps short and jerky.

"Ah, but that's where you're wrong." He fell into step beside her. "You're my responsibility until I report back to Bill."

"This is absolutely ridiculous." She turned away from him without waiting for a reply. Ignoring him, she forgot the elevator and stomped up the four flights of stairs that led to her apartment. She fumbled with her keys, flushing as they skittered to the floor. She fumed inwardly as he picked them up and put the correct key in the lock, unlatching the door and swinging it open.

He bowed gallantly. "Now my job is officially done. The lady is safely home."

"Good riddance," Libby exclaimed, stepping into her apartment. She stifled an outcry as she viewed the chaos that greeted her. "What's going on?" she cried, unable to comprehend the shambles in her apartment.

"What?" Tony stepped in, took one look at the mess, then quickly shoved her behind him.

Libby opened her mouth to complain of his rude treatment, then gasped as she realized a gun had somehow materialized in his hand.

"Stay behind me," he commanded in a whisper, taking another step into the ransacked apartment. "Whoever did this may still be in here."

Stay behind him? If Libby had the ability, she would have instantly become melded to his backside. "Tony...that's a gun," she squeaked inanely, her body pressed tightly against his back.

"Shh," he hissed, taking another awkward step forward, shadowed by Libby's leg, which moved as if joined to his.

They moved like this throughout the apartment, checking every corner, every closet. As they crept past the dresser mirror in the bedroom, she had an irresistible urge to giggle. They looked like an old-time vaudeville act in a bizarre dance without music. It was the look on Tony's face that kept her giggle trapped deep within her. Gone was the easy, lazy amusement she'd come to identify with him. His facial features were now tensed with the cold, calculated look of a man accustomed to coping with dangerous situations. His eyes were dark orbs, glittering with detail-consuming observation.

"It's okay, there's nobody here," he said, lowering the gun that had been leading their way around the small apartment.

"Are you sure?" she whispered, still clinging to his back like a baby koala bear to its mother.

"I'm positive," he answered, then grinned. "Besides, I'm beginning to enjoy this a little too much."

Libby blushed hotly and quickly stepped back from him, suddenly aware of how her full breasts had pushed insistently into his firmly muscled back.

A violent trembling seized her body as she looked at the ruins surrounding her. She wandered around, touching an item here and there, moaning as she saw her cherished possessions broken, torn apart, destroyed. The entire apartment had been thoroughly gone over, nothing left untouched. She turned tortured eyes to Tony. "Why?" she breathed softly. "What in the hell is going on?"

He shrugged, having no answers. Unable to control her spasmodic trembling, she stumbled to the sofa, her breaths coming in shallow, quick gasps. She was numb, stricken by the fact that she'd been violated not once, but twice in the same day.

She watched dully as Tony wandered around the apartment. She followed his gaze, noting the way the television had been gutted, the chair cushions slashed. In the kitchen, the drawers had been pulled out and emptied onto the floor. The cabinet doors hung open, their interiors showing signs of riffling.

"It looks like somebody was searching for something," Tony said.

"But what? I don't have anything of value." She felt

a hysterical giggle bubble to her lips. "Some of the furniture might be valuable to an antique collector, but nothing was taken...at least nothing I can see."

"Hmm," Tony murmured thoughtfully. He disappeared into the kitchen and returned a moment later carrying a tall glass of cold water. He held it out to her.

She took the glass from him, her throat scratchy and sore from the ache of suppressed tears.

"We need to talk," he said, his eyes searching her face thoughtfully.

She merely nodded, wondering what there was to talk about. She certainly had no answers for the craziness of the day.

"I think it's fairly obvious that the break-in at the pawnshop and this one are somehow connected." He began to pace in front of her. "It seems curious to me that nothing was stolen from the shop. It's filled with televisions, stereos, VCRs and such, yet the only thing you could find missing was your daily ledger."

"But the police seemed to think that the thieves must have been interrupted before they could take anything. Or that it was kids and the ledger was taken by mistake or thrown away."

"I can't buy either of those explanations, especially now. It's too much of a coincidence that both your pawnshop and this apartment have been broken into." He stopped pacing and looked at her once again, his dark gaze so piercing, he seemed to be trying to see into her very soul. "What could they have been looking for?"

"How should I know?" she asked. "I told you before, I don't have anything of real value. Certainly nothing worth all this trouble."

"Somebody apparently thinks you do."

"That's their problem," she retorted tiredly.

"For the moment, it seems to be your problem," he returned. "That pawnshop of yours... You haven't borrowed any money from anyone lately...you don't happen to have any high-finance backers or anything like that?"

For a moment she stared at him incredulously. "Are you asking me if I have a connection to organized crime? Don't be ridiculous." She eyed him with a sudden misgiving. "How do I know you don't have something to do with this? My life was very quiet and manageable until you began following me." Her gaze narrowed suspiciously.

"I guess we'll just have to trust each other," he finally said with staid calmness.

"Guess so," she quietly agreed after a long moment, too tired to sustain her suspicions and realizing Tony's involvement in this mess made no more sense than her own involvement.

As exhausted as she was, she roused herself from the couch, unable to stand the disorder around her for another moment.

"We should call the police and report this," Tony said, picking up a Navajo blanket from the floor.

"No. I don't want them here," she protested, pointing to where the blanket had been hanging on the wall. "I don't want anyone else pawing through my things, poking into my life." She shrugged. "Besides, what could they do? Ask me a million questions, then tell me it was the work of bored kids or dope addicts." She was aware that her voice sounded as hollow as she felt. She returned to the cleanup work, not even protesting as he began to work alongside her.

"I guess I'm going to owe you another meal," she said, trying to smile in spite of her chilled fatigue.

He smiled at her, a touch of humor back in his ebony eyes. "I have a feeling that before this is all over, you're going to owe me a hell of a lot more than just a meal."

Chapter 3

Despite Libby's protests, Tony insisted the police be called and a report filed. The officers arrived, looked around, made their report, then left.

Libby and Tony worked on the cleanup long after total darkness had fallen outside. They spoke very little, but the silence between them was a companionable one.

Twilight made an appearance, taking an instant dislike to Tony. The big tomcat crawled out from his hiding place beneath the couch, hissed and spat and spent the rest of the evening sitting on his hook rug staring unblinkingly at Tony.

Libby's anger deepened as they worked, and she realized that many of her things could not be repaired, but would have to be replaced. The television set was destroyed, as were the stereo and any other mechanical items she owned. The chair and sofa would have to be re-covered as deep rents had been slashed into them. The mattress on her bed would also have to be replaced. It had been cut and much of the filling had been pulled out.

Again and again Libby asked herself what kind of animals had been in her apartment. What could they have possibly been searching for with such vicious intensity? She was nearly overcome with exhaustion and bewilderment when she and Tony finally collapsed on the sofa, the worst of the mess straightened up.

"Thanks for all your help. It would have taken me all night to clean by myself." She wrinkled her brow thoughtfully. "It's just too bad we didn't find any clues to help solve this mystery." She looked at her watch and gasped. It was after ten o'clock. She pulled herself off the sofa. "Why don't you just sit tight and relax for a few minutes and I'll fix us a pot of coffee? I'd say we earned it."

Tony nodded wearily.

"The coffee will just take a minute," Libby called from the kitchen. She opened her refrigerator, wishing she'd bought some sort of cake or something suitable to serve with coffee. The only thing she had plenty of was cans of Twilight's stinky cat food, and somehow that didn't seem the proper thing to serve as a snack. She leaned against the counter tiredly, waiting impatiently for the dark brew to finish dripping through the filter.

In the living room, Tony settled back on the sofa. God, he was exhausted. He'd spent a miserable night in the cramped confines of his car, and the last thing he'd expected from the day was to be handed a mystery.

The search that had taken place both at the pawnshop and here had been total and complete, nothing left untouched. What was being sought? And was Libby as innocent in all this mess as she professed to be? It was a question his tired brain couldn't answer. Still, innocent or not, there was something about her that challenged him, stimulated him. His back still burned from the feeling of her soft breasts pressed tightly against him.

He'd been acutely aware of her as they'd worked together to clean up the apartment. The rooms had smelled of her, a feminine scent that conjured up visions of perfumed breasts, soft thighs and evocative heat. Dangerous thoughts, he cautioned himself, stifling a yawn with the back of his hand, wishing she'd hurry up and get the coffee out here so he could drink a cup and get the hell home.

"Here we go," Libby said moments later as she carried a bamboo serving tray in from the kitchen. She stopped short at the sight of Tony stretched out on her sofa, sound asleep. She set the tray down on the coffee table, thought about waking him, then changed her mind and instead took the opportunity to study him in his sleep.

Why is it that men look so vulnerable in sleep? she wondered, noticing the way his dark hair was tousled boyishly and most of the lines in his face disappeared in total relaxation. She flushed slightly, noticing that his shirt had ridden up, exposing part of his tanned, flat abdomen.

Her body felt curiously warm and heavy as her gaze slowly traveled down the length of him. She could imagine the firm muscles of his chest beneath his shirt, the perfect symmetry of his male physique. She pressed her hands to her sides, fighting the impulse to reach out and trace with her fingertips the exposed skin of his stomach.

She recognized the emotion sweeping over her, even though it had been a very long time since she'd last felt it. Lust. She grinned, realizing that the hormones she'd nearly forgotten she possessed were kicking in with a force that was breathtaking. Lust…desire…it was ridiculous. Her pawnshop had been ransacked, her apartment broken into and she was standing in the middle of her living room floor gazing at a sleeping man and feeling like a sexually peaking woman who finds herself on a deserted island with a handsome hunk. She stifled a hysterical giggle and reached out to shake Tony awake. Before her hand could make contact with his shoulder, he twitched. She recognized the movement as the muscle spasm of a man who was totally and completely exhausted.

Under normal circumstances, she would never allow a relative stranger to spend the night on her sofa.

But these were not normal circumstances. In the past twenty-four hours her world had been turned topsy-turvy. Besides, there was a certain amount of comfort in knowing she would not be alone in the apartment.

She turned out the lights in the kitchen and living room, then went into the bathroom.

As she took off her clothes, her mind whirled with questions. She agreed with Tony's assessment that whoever had broken into the pawnshop and here had been looking for something—but what? She racked her brain, seeking any answer that would make some sort of rational sense. But there were no answers forthcoming. She could only hope that they, whoever they were, had found what they were looking for, or realized she didn't have it.

She threw her clothes into the hamper, then pulled on the oversize velour robe that hung on a hook on the back of the bathroom door. She shoved her jewelry into the pocket of the robe and quickly washed her face.

Ready for bed, she left the bathroom, pausing at the door of her bedroom. "Come on, Twilight," she whispered to the cat, who was still curled up on the hook rug, eyeing the sleeping Tony suspiciously. "Come on, kitty," she called again, but Twilight studiously ignored her. "All right, then just stay out there," she murmured, going into her bedroom.

Always before upon entering the room, she'd felt as if she were entering a safe, warm retreat from the world. This time, the room seemed cold and alien. Even beneath the clean sheets now on the bed, the rips in the mattress could be seen. Elsewhere in the room there was further evidence of the massive search that had gone on while she had been away.

"Damn them," she said dispiritedly, taking off the robe and slipping into the blue teddy that was her sleeping attire.

"Damn them," she repeated, this time more forcefully. The room even smelled like something or someone strange had been in it. She crossed the small room and opened the window, breathing deeply of the cool, night air. She had no apartment insurance, having checked into it and found the premiums more than her budget could afford. She would have to replace the ruined items one at a time, as money allowed.

She sighed, finding it all overwhelmingly depressing. Overcome with a wave of tiredness, she crawled into bed, shivering slightly as her slender body attempted to get comfortable against the now-unfamiliar lumpy mattress. She shut off the bedside lamp and sighed again. What the hell was happening to her life?

Libby awoke suddenly to find a huge hand shoved over her mouth. Her eyelids fluttered open and in those first split seconds of instant awakeness, her mind registered several things. First was the fact that her bedroom window was now wide open. Secondly, she was intensely conscious of the man leaning over her, his hand clamped harshly against her mouth to still any scream that might touch her lips. Although the room was too dark for her to see anything except a bulky silhouette, she could smell him, a scent of sour perspiration and danger. The last realization that struck her was that she was in trouble. Her heartbeats came fast and furious as she struggled impotently against the big man who held her down against the bed.

"Where is it?" his guttural voice demanded.

Even in her terror, a ridiculous thought struck her. How did he expect her to answer his question when he had his grimy hand shoved halfway down her throat? Following on the heels of this thought came anger, a growing rage that took precedence over her fear.

How dare this slimy creature come into her bedroom in the middle of the night and place his filthy hand against her mouth, demanding answers to questions she didn't even begin to understand?

Instinctively she fought back the only way possible. She bit down on his hand as hard as she could, immediately tasting the coppery tanginess of blood. The man staggered backward, away from the bed with a strangled cry of pain. Mouth free, Libby let loose an ear-piercing scream.

Her bedroom door exploded open as Tony burst into the bedroom. The intruder, with a muttered curse, quickly crawled through the bedroom window and disappeared.

Libby scrambled for the bedside lamp, relief coursing through her as the bedroom was instantly illuminated. She turned to see Tony climbing out the window in hot pursuit.

She swiped at her mouth with the back of her hand, still able to taste the salty texture of the stranger's skin. She eyed the window in trepidation, wondering what was happening. Where was Tony? What was going on?

As she sat anxiously waiting, she became conscious of sounds in the apartment. The drip-drip-drip of the bathroom faucet. The loud hum of the refrigerator from the kitchen. Her digital clock radio clicked off each minute that passed. Where was Tony? Why was he taking so long to return? Had he caught up with the intruder? Were they at this very moment struggling on the dark streets outside?

A cold knot of terror formed in the pit of her stomach and she clenched her hands tightly until her nails entered her palms.

She jumped and screamed as a loud report echoed in the night. Oh, God, was it a gunshot? Or was it simply a car backfiring? Was Tony at this very moment lying in the street wounded…or worse…? What was happening? *What was happening?*

Her eyes widened in fear as she heard steady footsteps climbing up the fire escape outside the bedroom window. Frantically, she looked around for something that could be used as a weapon. She grabbed a heavy brass candlestick and hefted it over her head, frozen as the footsteps came closer and closer to the bedroom window.

She expelled a sob of relief and dropped the candlestick to the floor as Tony stepped back through the window. "Tony…I was so afraid…" She scrambled off the bed and came to stand next to him, her face blanching as she saw his torn shirt and the bright red blood that slowly trickled down his chest. "Oh…you're bleeding," she gasped. "Are you shot? Sit down. Should I call for an ambulance?"

"Libby." His sharp voice cut through her rising hysteria. "Sit down," he commanded, the thunder in his voice causing her knees to buckle beneath her. She fell onto the edge of the bed.

He tucked his gun back into the top edge of his boot and wiped at the bright trickle of blood with the back of his hand. "I am not hurt." He enunciated each word precisely. "Unless cat scratches have suddenly become life-threatening wounds."

She looked at him blankly. "Cat scratches?"

He nodded. "When you screamed, that wildcat you own took a flying leap from the rug to the sofa, landing on me with all claws bared."

Libby breathed a tremulous sigh of relief. "At least Twilight has had all his shots." She looked at the angry wounds on his chest and stood up from the bed. "But those should at least be cleaned out with some peroxide. Come on into the bathroom."

She led him into the bathroom, where she motioned for him to take off his shirt and sit down on the edge of the tub. She then grabbed some cotton balls and a bottle of peroxide.

"What happened to the man?" she asked, trying to keep her mind off the smooth firmness of his chest beneath her fingertips, off the attractive wild male scent that emanated from him.

"He got away." Tony's dark eyebrows slanted into a frown. "He jumped into a car that was waiting for him at the end of the street. What, exactly, happened before I got into your room?"

"I woke up to a hand shoved across my mouth and a guy asking, 'Where is it?'" She grimaced, remembering the feel of the man's hand against her lips.

"That's all he said?" Tony asked tersely, waving her

away impatiently and striding back into the bedroom where he began to pace back and forth in agitation.

She nodded and followed him into the bedroom. "Who are these people and what do they want from me?" The question was directed more to herself than at him.

"How the hell should I know?" Tony retorted impatiently. "It's you they're after, or at least something you have—but of course you have no idea what any of this is all about."

She reacted violently to the ill-concealed sarcasm that was heavy in his voice. "I don't have any idea what this is all about. I don't know what that man wanted from me." Her eyes narrowed. "Besides, you're the detective around here—you're supposed to be trained to deal with all sorts of criminals. That man crept into my room and could have done God-knows-what to me. If I hadn't managed to scream, you would have slept through the whole thing," she finished indignantly.

Tony's eyes turned black, dazzling with fury. "I didn't know you'd be stupid enough to leave the window open right next to the fire escape. Why didn't you just send them an engraved invitation for them to break in again?"

For a moment they stared at each other, their anger and frustration a living, breathing presence between them. It was Tony who finally broke the silence, shaking his head as if to steady himself. "This is getting us nowhere fast." His expression was a mask of stone, virtually unreadable. "We're both tired and overwhelmed by what's happened." He paused thoughtfully, then continued, "I think the thing to do is get you out of here right away."

"Don't be ridiculous. I'm not going to let some creep

force me out of my own home,'' she returned, eyeing him defiantly.

In one swift motion, his powerful hands grabbed her and pulled her to him. His eyes were hard and cold as he gazed down at her, and her body began to tremble against him.

''This is not a game, Libby. This is not the time to be stubborn and indignant. These men are professionals and those were real bullets they fired at me. They want something from you, and until we figure out what it is, you aren't safe. They know where you live—they've been here twice already. They'll be back. You're in danger here. Do you understand?''

She nodded numbly, unable to speak as her throat was achingly dry. She was suddenly very much aware of the fact that her scantily clad body was pressed tightly against his. She could feel his heartbeat against her skin, smell the rich maleness of him all around her. She was in danger here. Yes, she felt the danger, but she didn't know if at this very moment she was more afraid of the unknown men who wanted something from her, or the fire she saw in Tony's eyes—a smoldering flame that promised an intoxicating heat.

He dropped his arms from around her and stepped back. ''Get a bag together. We're getting out of here.'' His voice was hoarse. He turned and went into the living room, leaving her to stare numbly after him.

For a moment Libby stood unmoving, a tumble of confusion and emotions assailing her. It had been a long time since she'd felt any stirrings of sexual desire, but twice in a single evening Tony had managed to remind her that she was a normal woman with a normal woman's wants and needs.

''Okay, so you're human,'' she muttered, rousing herself from the lethargy that had momentarily gripped her. That didn't mean she was anxious to follow through on the sparks of desire that had arced between Tony and herself. After all, she hardly knew the man and wasn't even sure she liked him.

She quickly grabbed a few items from her closet and bathroom and shoved them into a suitcase. As she dressed, she kept her mind carefully schooled with numbness. She was unable to comprehend the forces that were driving her from her home, and unwilling to dwell on the force that crackled the air between herself and the man in the next room.

With a final look around the bedroom, she grabbed her suitcase and walked out.

Tony was pacing the living room floor, his movements as agile and lithe as a leopard's. He'd pulled his shirt back on, effectively hiding the smooth skin that had earlier tormented her. He turned as she entered the room and his mouth curved into a tight smile. "Ready?"

She nodded, clutching her suitcase tightly in her hand, wondering what they were going to do, where they were going to go. Was she a fool to trust this man? What did she know of him really? What other choice did she have?

"Let's get out of here before we encounter any more unwelcome guests." He opened the apartment door, looking out to make sure nobody suspicious lurked in the darkened hallway. Libby started to leave the apartment, then turned back with a cry of dismay. "Twilight. What am I going to do about Twilight?" She looked at Tony helplessly. "I can't just leave him here all alone."

Tony sighed with resignation and touched the scratches on his chest. "I guess we'll have to bring him along," he said unhappily.

With a grateful look, she handed him her suitcase, then called to the cat, who had taken refuge beneath the sofa earlier. The cat came willingly to Libby, who scooped him up in her arms and followed Tony out the apartment door.

"I feel like I picked up a mystery novel to read and skipped the first four chapters," she exclaimed as they rode the elevator down to the first floor.

"I sure wish you'd go back and read those chapters so we'd know exactly what we're dealing with," Tony returned wryly.

They didn't speak again until they were in his car. "Where are we going?" she asked, buckling her seat belt.

"My place. You'll be safe there."

Libby stroked the cat in her lap. Yes, she supposed she would be okay at his place. At least the people who were after her wouldn't know where she was. But safe? She remembered that moment in her bedroom when Tony's eyes had flamed with the fire of something much different than anger. Her body had responded with a warmth of its own, as if wanting to match his heat.

Safe? She wondered just how safe she really would be.

Chapter 4

"How far is it to your place?" Libby asked curiously as the car got underway. She tried to imagine the kind of apartment where he lived. It was probably a typical bachelor's pad, furnished with ultramodern furniture and the latest in stereo equipment. It was funny—there was no doubt in her mind that he was single, although he hadn't actually said he wasn't married. Yet she knew with a certainty there was no little lady keeping the fires warm at home.

"My place is about twenty minutes away. I live on the south side of Kansas City," he explained.

"Tony, if I knew what these people wanted from me, I'd tell you. Heck, I'd just give it to them. But I honestly don't know what this is all about," she said, unable to forget the doubt she'd sensed in his voice earlier.

"I know that," he replied after a moment's hesitation.

They fell silent, each disappearing into their own thoughts as they headed for his house. "Home, sweet home,'' he said as he turned down the street of a quiet, darkened neighborhood. He maneuvered the car into the driveway of a split-level house. With the push of a control button, the garage door rose. He pulled the car into the garage and together, Twilight, Tony and Libby got out of the car and entered a door that led into a small kitchen.

"You'll have to excuse the mess." He gestured rather sheepishly to the dirty dishes that were stacked up in the kitchen sink. "I wasn't exactly expecting company."

"Please, don't apologize." She shook her head tiredly. "I'm just grateful to have a place to sleep undisturbed." She hardly noticed the living room they passed through as he led her up the five stairs that went to the bedrooms.

"You can sleep in here," he said, placing her suitcase on the bed in what appeared to be a little used, spare bedroom. "I'll be right in the next bedroom if you need anything...." His dark eyes twinkled. "Or if you just want to snuggle."

"Twilight makes a very good snuggle partner," she returned lightly. He shrugged in mock resignation. Then, nodding a good-night, he left the room, closing the door behind him.

"Oh, Twilight, he's a smooth one," Libby murmured softly as she set the cat down on the edge of the bed. Twilight meowed as if in agreement. Yes, Tony Pandolinni was definitely a smooth operator, she thought as she quickly shrugged out of the large sweatshirt and jeans, eyeing the mattress longingly.

She turned off the bedroom light and crawled beneath the sheets of the unfamiliar bed. She yawned, smiling as she felt Twilight curl up at her feet. Yes, Tony had the capacity to be tremendously charming. It was a charm she assumed came quite naturally to him. But she also had a feeling it was one he took for granted, one that held little substance. She had a feeling that Tony Pandolinni gave his charm quite easily, but would give his heart much more grudgingly. Not that she cared, she reasoned sleepily. All she wanted was to straighten out this mystery and get back to her own life.

Tony changed out of his clothes and pulled on a robe, then went downstairs to the living room to sit and unwind. He knew from past experience that it would be some time before the adrenaline quit pumping through his veins and he could settle down to get some much-needed sleep.

He turned on the table lamp beside the sofa and was satisfied when the room lit with the warm glow of the low-watt bulb.

Libby... His expression turned thoughtful as he lit a cigarette and settled back on the sofa. What could she possibly possess that was so important? She certainly wasn't wealthy; her living conditions ruled out the possibility of a simple burglary. No, he was smart enough to recognize the signs of a search, and both the pawnshop and her apartment had undergone a massive one. Whatever it was they had been looking for, it had to be something very important to somebody.

His eyes narrowed even more as he remembered the bullet that had been directed at him. It was an intriguing puzzle, one that he was determined to put together. He dismissed the idea that her ex-husband was involved. Although the man was obviously besotted with Libby, and obsessed with getting her back into a marriage, he was far too pathetic to be able to put together this kind of thing.

He stirred restlessly on the sofa, his thoughts still on the woman upstairs in his spare room. Those eyes, those beautiful sapphire eyes. A man could melt into those blue depths, or he could be pulled up short by the strength and determination that lingered there. Most women would have completely fallen apart under the circumstances, yet Libby had remained firmly in control. There was more to the lady than met the eye, and this somehow pleased Tony.

He leaned his head back and closed his eyes for a moment, remembering that instant in her apartment when he had pulled her tightly against him. It had been the first moment when he'd noticed that her attire was less than modest. The blue teddy did little to hide the rounded curves of her breasts and slender hips, the silky length of her long legs. He'd been shocked at the unexpected flare of desire that ripped through him, a desire that was completely unwanted.

He stubbed out his cigarette, looking up as he heard a door open upstairs. Libby appeared at the top of the stairs.

"Can't sleep?" he asked, noting how small and vulnerable she looked as she stood hesitantly, clad in her oversize robe. Her pale hair was tousled like a halo around her head, attesting to the fact that she had tossed and turned restlessly.

"No. I'm totally exhausted, but I can't seem to wind down enough to sleep." She self-consciously smoothed the front of her robe, pulling the belt tighter around her slender waist. "Would you mind if I joined you?"

"Not at all," he agreed easily, watching her grace as she walked down the stairs and sat down in the chair across from him.

"This is all so bizarre," she began hesitantly, fingering the fringe at the end of the robe's belt. She sighed tiredly. "I'm sitting in the living room of a man I hardly know because somebody is after me for something I have, only I don't know what that something is—" She broke off with a deep sigh of frustration. "I'm so tired, but the minute I lay down on the bed, all kinds of questions start playing in my mind." She smiled ruefully. "Twilight didn't have the same problem. He curled up in a ball on the bed and immediately fell asleep."

Tony grinned his easy smile. "We should all have the adaptability of animals." He smiled at her again, suddenly making her conscious of the intimacy of their setting. The soft, warm lighting...both of them in bathrobes. Anyone peeking in the windows at the moment would have guessed them to be a married couple, or perhaps lovers. Certainly nobody would guess they were relative strangers thrown together by a series of events that were out of their control.

"How about a drink?" Tony suggested. "I'd offer you a glass of wine. Physically you look like a wine sipper, but something tells me that look is probably deceptive." He smiled teasingly. "Let me guess, you probably can knock back ten Scotches on the rocks without blinking an eye."

"Actually, I'm a tequila drinker from way back," she admitted, finding it impossible not to respond to his light tone.

His eyebrows shot up in surprise at her answer. "Whew! You're a better man than I, Libby." His grin was infectious and Libby felt herself responding with a warmth that coursed through her veins as he continued. "I'm afraid I don't have any tequila, but I can offer you some nice, smooth brandy."

"That sounds great," she agreed, a smile lingering on

her lips as she watched him rise from the sofa and disappear into the kitchen. Did he know how potent his smile was?

Probably, she reasoned. Men who looked like Tony Pandolinni were rarely unaware of their charm. It would be easy to be drawn into the magic of it, but that was something she wasn't about to do. She was finally getting her life back together, learning to be alone again. She wasn't interested in jumping into another relationship, especially not with a smooth operator like Tony.

She looked around the room, for the first time noticing her surroundings. Unlike the bachelor pad she had first imagined, there was very little in the room to attest to the character of the man who lived here. All the furnishings were basic, nondescript, earth tones. The pictures on the wall would have been as much at home in any impersonal motel room. There were no books, no knickknacks, no photographs—nothing to reveal the character of the man residing here. She frowned pensively, once again aware that she had placed her safety, her very life into the hands of a man she knew nothing about.

"Here you go."

She looked up as Tony reentered, holding two glasses of the amber liquid. He handed her a glass, then resumed his half-prone position on the sofa. She took a sip of the brandy, feeling the warmth of the alcohol caressing her insides. She looked at him reflectively. "I was just thinking about how little your home tells about you. I really don't know anything about you."

He shrugged and sipped his drink. "There isn't much to tell."

"Were you hatched, or do you have a family?" she

asked lightly, needing conversation to keep away thoughts of boogeymen in the night.

He laughed. "My father is Italian, hot-blooded and temperamental, and my mother was Irish, very emotional. They always told me that I'm the product of their worst attributes." For a moment his face darkened, as if a storm cloud had drifted momentarily in front of the sun. "So, tell me about owning a pawnshop," he said, smoothly turning the topic of conversation away from himself.

"Did you know that owners of pawnshops are in the high-risk category for being junk-food junkies?" She laughed at his look of surprise. "It's true. Every pawnstore owner I've ever known is a sucker for greasy hamburgers and potato chips."

"I'd quit the business before I'd allow a fate like that to befall me," Tony exclaimed.

"Oh, no," she protested. "That's exactly why I got into the business. When I discovered my love for junk food, I knew what my professional calling would be."

"You like being in the business," he observed.

"I love it," she replied, sipping her brandy and leaning back in the chair.

"I'd think it would be sort of sad, to see people bringing in their things to be pawned."

"Sometimes it can be rather sad," she agreed. "But my shop has a high ratio of people who come back to reclaim their items. I like to think of my shop as a friend for my customers, a friend who will make loans when times are tough." She finished her drink and set the empty glass on the coffee table next to her. "So, tell me about your private-eye business."

He winced. "At the moment, there's very little to tell.

It's all still pretty new and like any young business, it's going to take time to get on its feet.''

"What made you decide to quit the police department?" she asked, smiling apologetically as she stifled a yawn with the back of her hand.

He shrugged, getting up off the sofa and wandering to the window where he peered out into the darkness of the night. "My father was a cop...retired off the force with thirty years' street experience." He frowned, thinking of all the things he could tell her...but wouldn't. "He encouraged me to follow in his footsteps, join the force. I did. For eleven years I worked the streets, got promoted from traffic cop to Homicide. I worked, ate and slept the job." Again he frowned, shoving back old, painful memories. "I just got tired of the paperwork, decided I wanted to be my own boss. So, here I am." He paused a moment, waiting for some sort of response from her. When none was forthcoming, he turned to look at her, a rueful smile curving his lips as he realized she was sound asleep.

For a long time he simply stood there staring at her, trying to find a single physical trait he didn't like. There were none. Everything about her appealed to him, the dainty features, the firm, stubborn chin, the pale gold angel hair that was tousled carelessly around her face. He could admire her beauty, enjoy her strength and sense of humor, but that was as far as it would go. He'd made a vow long ago that he would never share his life with any woman on a permanent basis, and it was a vow he intended to keep, no matter how attractive the woman might be.

He touched her shoulder gently. "Libby," he whispered in an effort to wake her and send her off to bed. She stirred, but didn't waken. He thought about leaving her in the chair to sleep, but knew that in the morning she'd be cramped and sore from the awkward sleeping position.

With a sigh of resignation, he gently scooped her up into his arms. His heart thudded erratically as, in her sleep, her arms sought out and clung around his neck. He carried her up the stairs to the bedroom, trying to ignore the sweet fragrance that emanated from her, the feminine curves that pressed against him.

He gently deposited her on the bed, his breath catching in his throat as the robe she wore gaped open and he spied a teasing glimpse of blue lace and creamy skin.

Ignoring the cat, who hissed a warning, he covered her with the sheet. He turned to leave the room, then paused a moment, staring at her. What could she possibly possess that somebody would want so badly? Why the ransacking of both the pawnshop and her apartment? There was a scent of danger surrounding her, and Tony wondered how to fight an unknown enemy who had mysterious motives.

Hawk sat alone in the all-night café, sipping a cup of stale, thick coffee and cursing the Fates that had brought him to this hole-in-the-wall eatery.

He looked at his wristwatch, then popped an antacid tablet into his mouth, hoping it would work its magic against the acidic burning in the pit of his stomach.

He frowned, wondering why these meetings were always set up in fly-infested, filthy cafés and bars. Even as the question crossed his mind, he dismissed it, knowing the answer. Most of the men who worked with him and for him were living on the edge. They were hardened criminals, seasoned mercenaries, men who owed their loyalties only to the people who paid the highest dollar amount. They were men without conscience, men who would do anything to anyone if the price was right. But they were also men who shied from the bright lights of public places, men who preferred the shadows of little frequented spots of a city.

And so here he sat in the gloom of the squalid café, growing more and more agitated as minutes grew into hours. He gestured for more coffee and popped another antacid tablet from the roll in his pocket.

As the sullen, disinterested waitress refilled his coffee cup, Hawk's frown deepened. He was irritated that the attempt to get the item from Libby Weatherby had been bungled. However, no one had anticipated the possibility of a man being in the apartment with her.

Hawk's eyes darkened as he thought of the man who had not only thwarted their efforts in the woman's bedroom, but had also managed to spirit her away from them. He sipped his coffee with a grimace, thinking of the man who'd made the mistake of helping Libby Weatherby. Hawk would take great pleasure in dealing with the man himself. He would smile while he slit the man's throat.

He sat up straighter in the red vinyl booth as a tall albino man walked into the room. The albino's pale eyes swiftly swept the perimeters of the nearly empty café, then focused on Hawk.

He slid into the seat across from Hawk and stared at him enigmatically. Of all the men who worked for Hawk, this one made him the most uncomfortable. Perhaps because of all the men who worked for him, the albino was the most unpredictable, the most dangerous.

Hawk knew very little about the man, didn't even know his real name. What little he did know made him doubt the pale man's sanity, but he never questioned his cunning or instinct for survival.

The two men faced each other silently. The albino never spoke first, maintaining silence as a sign of power and control. Many times Hawk had challenged the muteness of the pale man, meeting silence with silence, but he'd always been the first one to grow uncomfortable and speak. This time he didn't even consider playing a game of power with the man. The stakes were much too high. Time was too precious to waste in such foolishness.

"Did you get the information I requested?" Hawk asked.

The albino shook his head. "We can't do anything until morning. Some of these things do take time."

"We don't have time," Hawk spat out angrily. "We not only don't know where the merchandise is, we don't even know where the girl is!"

"She will be found," the albino stated succinctly, his pale, pinkish eyes glittering with an unholy light Hawk found unnerving.

"She will have to be disposed of, but not until we have what we need from her." Hawk's voice was a mere whisper.

The albino nodded, no expression on his pale face. "I will see to it personally."

For a split second, Hawk almost felt sorry for Libby Weatherby. Her death would not be quick and clean. The albino never worked that way. Her death would be excruciatingly slow and painful.

"What of the man?" Hawk asked. After picking up their cohort, who'd snuck into the apartment, Hawk had doubled back just in time to see Libby and the man getting into a car. He'd been about to follow them, but had the misfortune of getting pulled over by a cruising patrol car who had seen him roll through a stop sign. At least he'd been able to get the license number of the car that had spirited Libby Weatherby away from her apartment.

"We'll know his name and address first thing in the morning," the albino assured him. "Our contacts in Motor Vehicles will get us the information we need. And then we'll take care of them both." For the first time, a smile lifted the albino's lips, sending a cold chill waltzing up and down Hawk's spine.

Chapter 5

Libby awoke slowly, disoriented, as she opened her eyes and viewed her surroundings. Fear tensed her body beneath the thin covers of the bed as she looked around the room blankly. Where was she? The light of dawn was just creeping over the horizon, letting her know it was very early. Then, as she felt the familiar, heavy weight of Twilight at her feet, she remembered. She was in Tony Pandolinni's spare bedroom.

She remained in the bed for a few minutes, rerunning the previous day's events in her mind. The pawnshop... her apartment...the man in her bedroom... It all whirled around, dizzying and confusing. What in God's name had happened to her safe and orderly life? She was in a stranger's bedroom, driven here by circumstances she didn't understand. And what was really strange was that Tony didn't seem like a stranger. At that moment Libby felt like he was the only sanity in a world gone crazy.

Oh, she should have never drunk that glass of brandy the night before. The smooth warmth of the drink on top of her empty stomach had combined with her confusion to put her out like a light. Heat suffused her as she vaguely recalled being lifted into strong arms and laid gently onto the bed. Thank heavens Tony Pandolinni was a gentleman, because she had a feeling that the combination of the alcohol and her fear would have made her vulnerable to the touch of his lips against hers, the warmth of his hand against her breast. And that was a complication she didn't need in her life at the present time.

She took a deep, refreshing breath, then bounded from the bed with a burst of energy, pulling fresh clothes from the small overnight bag and laying them on the bed.

In the soft light of the morning, with the brilliant bird songs filtering through the window and a soft breeze blowing the lacy curtains, it would have been easy to minimize the events of the previous day. However, Libby was no fool, and she was not particularly comforted by the normalcy promised in the beauty of the new morning.

"What I want today is some answers," she said aloud to Twilight, who sat patiently at the closed bedroom door, drawn there by the scent of frying bacon wafting on the air. Tony was also up early. "We've got to find out what's happening," she continued, pulling on a pair of clean jeans, ignoring Twilight's *meow,* which sounded like a definite complaint. "We need to find out what those people want from me," she explained to the cat as she pulled a pale blue sweatshirt over her head, ignoring Twilight's impatient scratching on the closed door.

She removed a hairbrush from her suitcase and

quickly pulled it through her sleep-tousled hair as Twilight once again scratched insistently on the bedroom door. She replaced the hairbrush in her purse, then efficiently made the bed. "Okay, okay, I'm ready," she said to the cat, opening the bedroom door and allowing Twilight to dart out ahead of her and down the stairs.

"Ah, the killer beast has awakened." Tony's deep voice rang out pleasantly from the kitchen. "And the killer beast's fair mistress," he added, as Libby stepped into the kitchen.

"Good morning," Libby murmured, hesitantly, feeling unaccountably shy as she watched him puttering in the kitchen, apparently preparing a full, hearty breakfast. He wore a gray shirt, the sleeves rolled up to expose his strong, tanned forearms. And the worn jeans did little to hide the firm shape of his rear end. *It should be a crime to have a butt that looks that good in jeans,* she thought, a strange warmth coursing through her.

"Help yourself to the coffee." He smiled and gestured to the full pot of coffee that sat in the coffeemaker on the countertop. "The eggs will be ready in a jiffy."

"No eggs for me," Libby protested as she poured herself a cup of coffee and sat down at the glass-topped kitchen table. "I'm not much of a breakfast eater," she explained, noting how at home he looked in the kitchen. Obviously, he was a man accustomed to taking care of his own needs.

"Didn't anyone ever tell you that breakfast is the most important meal of the day?" His voice held a light, teasing note.

"Yes, for years my father made me eat breakfast. Then, when I got married, my husband insisted I cook his breakfast every morning. Now that I'm on my own, I don't even look at food before noon."

"Personally, I can skip any other meal of the day, but I have to have my breakfast." He grinned, turning back to the stove.

Libby sipped her coffee and watched as he expertly cracked several eggs into an awaiting skillet on the stove. "Perhaps after you've eaten you wouldn't mind dropping me off at the pawnshop?" she asked.

"Bad idea," he replied, transferring the eggs to a plate and moving the skillet off the burner. He joined her at the table. "Are you sure you don't want something?" he asked.

"No, really, coffee is just fine." Libby looked distastefully at the plate of heaping food before him.

He shrugged as if to indicate it was her loss, then dug in, eating with a gusto Libby found almost nauseating so early in the morning. "I don't want you anywhere near that shop until we find out what's going on," he explained between bites.

She thought about it, then slowly nodded her agreement. "Okay, then take me back to my apartment."

"An equally dangerous move." He lay down his fork and looked at her, his dark eyes grave and sober. "Libby, you'd be an absolute fool to dismiss lightly all that has happened to you. Those men were quite serious last night, and I can almost guarantee they will be just as serious this morning."

"So, what do you suggest? I can't stay here forever. I do have a life to get back to." She couldn't keep an edge of impatience out of her voice.

"Let me make some contacts. I've still got some good friends on the police force. Let me talk to them and see if they can give me some insight on all this."

"How are they going to know any more than we do?" she scoffed irritably. "They were the ones that told me the pawnshop was broken into by kids. And last night they said they thought maybe the apartment mess was the work of a gang. I'll tell you, it was no kid who crawled into my bedroom window last night.'' She shivered suddenly, remembering the feel of the man's hand against her mouth, the smell of his body, oppressive and rancid.

"Give me today.'' Tony reached across the table and captured one of her hands in his. Libby immediately felt a stir of warmth, an electric current connecting his hand to the pit of her stomach. She nodded, realizing she would agree to anything with his hand holding hers. She snatched her hand away and grabbed her coffee cup.

"Okay, I'll give you today, but if we don't come up with any answers, then I'm going home.''

Tony nodded and looked at his watch. "I've got a buddy who comes on duty at seven in the morning. I think I'll head on to the station and see if I can catch him.''

"What can I do to help solve this mystery?'' she asked, focusing on what was important, refusing to stop and analyze why the touch of his hand had affected her in a most pleasant fashion.

Tony stood up, a frown creasing his forehead. "I'm not sure, but because the pawnshop was the first place searched, I would say the answer to this puzzle somehow lies there.'' Libby nodded her agreement, realizing that at least that much made sense. "While I'm gone, I want you to make a list of everyone who came into the shop on the day before the break-in. Write down names and what items were pawned.''

This time it was Libby's turn to frown. "That's quite a tall order. This is the busiest time of the year for the business. Besides, there are lots of customers who I've never seen before and probably won't see again. I certainly won't be able to remember their names."

"Just do the best you can." He looked at his watch once again. "I've got to get out of here if I want to meet Cliff down at the station." With a quick smile, he was gone, leaving Libby with the impression that he had somehow taken some of the color out of the kitchen when he left.

She poured herself another cup of coffee and sat back down at the table, staring absently out the window that looked out into his large backyard.

Thank God Tony seemed to be a stand-up kind of a guy. Circumstances make strange bedfellows, she thought, then shook her head. The last thing she wanted was a bedfellow of any kind. Still, she couldn't deny the fact that she was attracted to Tony—attracted in a way that had her thinking of sultry nights, satin sheets and dangerous passion. It was crazy how those charcoal-flaming eyes of his made her remember the joy of making love, the fact that it had been a very long time since she'd indulged in that particular pleasure.

"Hormones," she said aloud, draining her coffee cup and taking it to the sink. What she was suffering was nothing more than the resurgence of hormones too long denied.

She was pulled from her thoughts by the plaintive *meows* of Twilight, who sat at her feet and looked up at her expectantly. Knowing the cat was demanding breakfast, she quickly placed a dish with the leftover bacon and eggs down on the floor.

Seeing that Twilight was content, she found a piece of paper and a pen, then sat back down at the table, realizing it was time to get to work on the business at hand. She needed to think of names and items pawned on the day before the break-in. She knew the quicker they solved her little mystery, the quicker she could get back to the sanity of her own life.

"Tony, I'd really like to help you, but I'm on my way out. We've got a stiff downtown in an alley."

"So, what else is new?" Tony asked wryly, grinning at the short, wiry man he considered his best friend.

Cliff didn't return his smile. "What's new is that this particular stiff is not the run-of-the-mill wino or junkie the downtown district normally turns up. Seems this guy was some sort of respected scientist until he wandered into the alley behind Bateman's Shoe Repair and caught a bullet through his head."

Tony's blood suddenly raced through his veins. Bateman's Shoe Repair was right next door to Libby's pawnshop. Coincidence? His nose told him there were just too many damned coincidences in all of this mess. "Cliff, let me ride with you. This might tie into something I've been working on."

Cliff frowned for a moment. "I don't know...we've got heavy brass leaning on our butt on this one."

"Come on, man," Tony said urgently. "I've got a gorgeous blonde waiting for some answers, and my nose tells me this might be the place to start looking for some of those answers."

"A gorgeous blonde, huh?" Cliff grinned in disbelief. He relented. "Okay, but make sure you stay out of the way."

As they drove to the scene of the murder, Cliff filled Tony in on the details that were known so far. "The body was discovered about an hour ago by the garbagemen who service the area. They moved the Dumpster and the body was behind it. They immediately called the police."

Tony looked out the passenger window of the patrol car and frowned as Cliff brought the car to a halt. He felt a funny feeling in the pit of his stomach as he saw the Dumpster, between the back door of Libby's place and the shoe repair store next door. Surely there was no connection...surely the unusual things happening to Libby and the death of this scientist were totally unrelated.

He tugged at his mustache thoughtfully, smelling something dirty, something discernible only to his nose. Most people relied on their gut reaction. Tony relied on his nose. When he'd been a cop and a case went awry, he could always smell it happening. And in this particular case, he definitely smelled something ugly. Now, if he could just figure out what exactly it was that stank.

Libby grimaced and scratched out a name she had just written on the sheet of paper before her. The job of trying to remember everyone who had come into the shop on a particular day was more difficult than she'd thought it would be. Without her ledger, she was lost.

She looked down at the sheet of paper with a sigh of dissatisfaction. She knew the list was incomplete, but it was difficult to try to reconstruct an entire day of business from memory alone.

She placed her chin in her hands, struggling with not only the elusive names of customers, but the millions of unanswered questions that whirled around and around in her head. She looked up, startled as Tony burst through the doorway. "That was quick," she exclaimed, noting by the kitchen clock that he had been gone less than an hour.

"Cliff was tied up with a murder case. Seems some sort of genius Defense Department scientist managed to get himself killed."

"Here in Kansas City?" she asked in surprise, getting up to pour him a cup of coffee as he sat down at the table. "What would a Defense Department scientist be doing here in Kansas City?"

"It seems this guy was something of an enigma. He worked for the Defense Department in a lab in Washington, D.C, for almost twenty years. Then, two years ago, he quit the department and left D.C., retiring to a private lab in the Ozarks. Word has it that he was still doing projects for the government." He nodded his thanks as she set the coffee cup before him, then rejoined him at the table. "From what Cliff was able to discover, he left the Ozarks area in a private plane on Tuesday, and arrived in Kansas City around nine o'clock, at which time he left the plane, instructing the pilot to be ready to take off again within an hour. He never made it back to the plane." He leaned forward and Libby suddenly noticed the tenseness of his body. "His body was found behind the Dumpster between your pawnshop and Bateman's Shoe Repair."

Libby felt a cold finger of fear reach inside and caress the inside of her stomach. "You...you don't think this has anything to do with me?" She paused a moment as he merely looked at her. "What...what was his name?"

"Jasper Higgens."

"Oh my God," she gasped.

"What?" Tony demanded.

"He was in my shop. Look, I have his name on my list." She shoved the list of names at him, pointing to the scientist's. "It was the first time he'd been in the shop, but I remembered his name because it was unusual, *he* was unusual.'' She gasped as another thought struck her. ''He was in my shop around nine-thirty. My God, Tony, he must have been killed immediately after leaving the pawnshop.'' She stared at Tony in horror.

Tony stumbled to his feet and took her by the shoulders. ''Think, Libby. This is very important. What did he bring into the shop? What did he pawn?''

''A necklace,'' she answered without hesitation. ''It was a gold necklace.''

''Where is it?''

''I...I don't know...at home,'' she answered in confusion, trying to remember where the necklace was at that precise moment. ''No, wait, it's here.'' She jumped up out of her chair and ran up the stairs and into the bedroom where she had slept the night before. She dug into her suitcase and pulled out her bathrobe, reaching into the pocket and breathing a sigh of relief as she felt the heavy gold of the necklace.

''Did you find it?''

She turned to see Tony standing in the doorway of the bedroom. She held the piece out to him wordlessly.

Tony took the necklace and scrutinized it closely. ''I'll admit, it's an attractive piece of jewelry. But surely it's not worth a man's life.'' He bent his head down closer to the necklace, his fingers moving over the thick centerpiece. ''This looks like a locket. Does it open?''

Libby shrugged. ''I don't really know. I didn't try to open it.'' She watched impatiently as he worked with the center in an effort to get it to open.

''Ah-ha,'' he said triumphantly as the locket sprang open. Then he frowned. ''It's empty.'' He closed the locket once again.

''What on earth could this necklace have to do with

any of this mess?'' she asked softly, her utter confusion evident in her voice.

"I'm not sure, but at this point I don't think we can discount the importance of it. There have been too many coincidences. A man comes into your pawnshop and leaves a necklace. He's murdered and later that night your shop is ransacked and your apartment is broken into.'' He shook his head thoughtfully. "I just can't help but think that somehow everything ties in with the necklace...but why?'' His brow wrinkled in perplexity. "Put this on. Until we know more, this necklace is the only thing we have to go on. At least with it around your neck, we'll know where it is.''

She nodded and turned around, allowing him to fasten the necklace at the nape of her neck. It snuggled against her skin, the feel of it giving her no pleasure at all. Before when she had worn the piece she had enjoyed the feel of the warm gold nestled against her skin. This time was different because she now knew there was a possibility that the necklace had been the cause of a man's death. That knowledge made it feel cold and alien against her flesh. She turned back to face Tony.

"Are you all right?'' he asked, his finger reaching up and lightly touching her cheek.

She nodded and forced a small smile to her lips. "Just a little overwhelmed by all this.''

"Come on, let's go back downstairs. I'm going to try to call Cliff and see if there's any more information.'' He placed an arm around her shoulders as together they went back down to the kitchen.

As Tony dialed the phone, Libby sank back down at the table. Before, her situation had seemed desperate—now it had taken on a new dimension. She reached up and touched the necklace around her throat. What secret could it possess that was so valuable it might have cost a man his life?

She turned her attention to Tony, who listened intently to somebody on the other end of the phone line. His sharply etched features were tense and his eyes were onyx orbs radiating intelligence. He looked like a man capable of handling danger. She certainly hoped so, for as she sat there watching while he scribbled something down on a notepad, she realized how very dependent she was on him at the moment.

"Whew." He expelled a low breath as he hung up the phone.

"What? What were you able to find out?" she asked anxiously.

"I just spoke to Cliff. The case of Jasper Higgens has been taken away from the police department and handed to another agency...one working on the assumption that national security may have been compromised."

Libby stared at him in amazement. "National security?" She emitted a squeak of unbelieving laughter. "What on earth could a necklace have to do with national security?"

"I don't know."

Libby released another burst of nervous laughter. "Two days ago I was simply an average pawnbroker, and now you're telling me it's possible that somehow I'm in the middle of some national security crisis." She breathed a shuddery sigh. "Couldn't we just give the necklace to somebody, you know, the FBI or the CIA?"

"I suppose we could," he said thoughtfully. "However, I'm extremely reluctant, especially when I don't know what's going on. I think we'd be better off finding out exactly why this necklace is so important before we just blindly hand it over to anyone."

"But how do we go about doing that?"

He shrugged and smiled. "We go to the Ozarks," he said succinctly.

"We go to the Ozarks...." she repeated blankly. "And what do we do once we get there?"

"We go to Jasper Higgens's lab, we talk to his associates. Surely he wasn't working completely alone. Then we find out exactly what he was working on...and maybe that will give us some answers to this whole puzzle."

"You're crazy," she exclaimed. "I say we just give the necklace to one of the people in the agency that's working on the case."

"Fine. We'll just hand it over to somebody on the task force, but you choose who we give it to. And let me warn you, you'd better make sure he's a patriotic, duty-bound guy who can't be swayed to the wrong side of the tracks by a flash of cash. You'd better make sure he can't be bought at any price and has no family who can be threatened, because if this necklace holds a secret that threatens the security of the United States, by handing it to the wrong person, you sell us all up the river." His voice rang with passion, and his dark eyes blazed with the full depth of his emotions.

"Out of all the ex-cops in the world, I've got to get stuck with a flag-waving, national anthem-singing patriot with altruistic motives, placing the burden of our country's freedom square on my shoulders." She glared at him, irritated that he had managed to present to her an argument she couldn't fight.

"Look, Libby, I'm not suggesting we handle all this alone from the beginning to the end. All I'm suggesting is that we learn more about everything before we make any final decisions about who to give the necklace to."

He tapped the end of his nose. "Some cops rely on their gut reaction. I always relied on my nose, and it's telling me to take all this very slow."

She stared at him for a long moment, noting the energy that radiated through him, the glint of anticipation that lit his eyes. He wants to do this, she thought in amazement.

She relented. "Okay, we go to the Ozarks and see what we can find out, but only on one condition."

"What?"

"If things get really dangerous and I feel like we're in over our heads, you'll call somebody in to help us."

"It's a deal." He smiled at her, the smile that always made her heart jump erratically in her chest. She suddenly found herself wondering if she wasn't already in over her head.

He got up and shut off the coffeemaker and looked at his watch. "It's almost nine o'clock now. If we get on the road right away we should get to the lab sometime this afternoon."

"I'm ready when you are," she said, placing their coffee cups in the sink. "Oh, what about Twilight? What are we going to do with him while we're gone?" she asked as the cat came into the kitchen and sat down at Tony's feet, staring up at him balefully.

Tony stared back at the big, gray tomcat, unconsciously rubbing his chest where the cat's claws had made contact with his skin the night before. Twilight meowed as if to protest the dastardly thoughts whirling around in Tony's head as he considered the fate of the cat. "We should be able to find out what we need and make it back sometime late tonight. Won't he be all right in the house until then?"

"I suppose so." She looked at Twilight fondly, silently amused at the way the cat's unblinking stare seemed to make Tony uncomfortable. "We'll need to leave him some food and water."

"Why don't you take care of that? Help yourself to whatever bowls and feline-type food you can find."

Libby nodded and smiled down at the cat as she quickly got him some water and a can of tuna. As she set the bowls down, she leaned over and petted him behind his ears. The large cat rolled over on his back, baring his furry belly to her gently scratching hand. "You're a sweet kitty," she murmured softly.

"If I roll over on my back, will you scratch my belly?" Tony asked with a wide smile.

Libby straightened up and eyed him levelly. "Has that kind of smooth flirting always come so easily to you?"

He winced. "Ouch. Are you always such a straight shooter?"

"Always. That's one thing my father taught me."

"What else did your father teach you?" he asked once they were in the car and on their way.

"He taught me how to bluff at poker, curse like a sailor and spit between my two front teeth, the latter of which I gave up upon reaching puberty."

Tony laughed. "He sounds like a hell of a guy."

"Oh, he is," she replied, warmed by thoughts of her father. "He retired to Florida a year ago and I miss him dreadfully."

Tony thought of his own father and tightened his grip on the steering wheel. He envied her the loving relationship she shared with her father. He'd spent years trying to develop something with his own old man. The desire to please Anthony Pandolinni, Sr., was what had prompted Tony to join the police force, but even that move couldn't bridge the distance between the two men.

He shoved these thoughts from his head, refusing to dwell on painful memories, old baggage. Instead he focused on the mystery at hand, surprised to feel the old familiar adrenaline kicking in at the challenge he sensed lay ahead. He hadn't felt this way since he'd left the force. "Damn!" he suddenly exploded, hitting the steering wheel with the palm of his hand.

"What's the matter?" Libby asked worriedly.

"I left the directions to Higgens's lab lying on the kitchen table."

"Should we turn around and go back for them?"

He thought for a moment. "No," he finally answered. "I think I can remember everything I wrote down."

She nodded and settled back in the seat.

Tony slowly began to relax as the monotony of highway driving overtook him and he realized Libby had fallen asleep. Small wonder...they had both been up late the night before and up this morning with the dawn.

He looked over at the sleeping woman, fighting an impulse to reach over and run a finger down the softness of her cheek, or trail his fingers through the pale blond hair that fell down to her shoulders. Her scent surrounded him, and like a bloodhound on the trail of a rabbit, it enticed him.

Once again he found his grip tightening on the steering wheel. Damn, what was the matter with him? He'd always prided himself on his ability to stay coolly detached from any emotional relationship with members of the opposite sex. What was it about Libby Weatherby that touched him in a way he'd never been touched before?

His thoughts were interrupted as Libby stirred in her sleep. His breath caught tightly in his chest as she turned toward him and her hand flopped over to rest softly on his upper thigh. He immediately felt a coil of heat ignite in the pit of his stomach. Damn, he scoffed inwardly. It was going to be a torturously long drive to their destination.

Hawk pulled his sports car to a stop by the curb in front of Tony Pandolinni's split-level house. Their contact in the Motor Vehicles department had finally gotten back to them with his address from the tag numbers Hawk had obtained.

"You can kill the P.I., but we need Libby Weatherby alive," he said to the man in the passenger seat. "We must have her alive to tell us what she's done with the necklace."

"And after she tells us?" the albino asked.

Hawk shrugged. "Then she's expendable." He ignored the albino's smile of anticipation. "Go check out the house and take care of business."

Hawk watched as the pale man slipped out of the car and walked down the sidewalk to the front door. In the three-piece suit, the man looked like nothing more than an irksome door-to-door salesman. Tony Pandolinni would innocently open the door before he looked into the pale man's eyes. And when he looked into those cold, colorless depths, he would see his own death there.

Hawk frowned as the albino knocked on the door for a third time. Finally, after looking back toward Hawk, the albino picked the lock and entered the house.

The minutes crept by as Hawk waited impatiently for the albino's return to the car. He hoped nothing went wrong. He had waited so long for the moment when the necklace would be finally in his possession. The scientist had been foolish to think he could escape. His death had been unfortunate, but necessary.

Hawk allowed a small smile to lift his heavy features as he thought of finally possessing the necklace. With the necklace, he would be the most powerful man on earth. What a rush.

He tensed as the front door reopened, then relaxed as the pale man came out and walked confidently to the car. Apparently everything was well under control. "Did you get it?" he demanded as the man got back into the car.

The albino shook his head negatively. "Nobody was home, but the coffeepot was still warm."

"Damn!" Hawk pulled his antacids out of his breast pocket and popped two in his mouth. "Where in the hell could they have gone?"

The albino broke into a full, ugly grin and held up a piece of paper. "They were kind enough to leave us directions."

Chapter 6

Libby awoke to find her head resting on Tony's shoulder, her hand lying intimately on his thigh. She jerked up and away from him as if scorched by the heat of a fire.

"Ah, Sleeping Beauty awakens." Tony smiled at her.

"I'm sorry," she said, running fingers through her hair self-consciously, trying not to think of how familiarly she'd been sleeping against him. "I guess I haven't been very good company."

"That's all right. You were obviously exhausted."

She focused her attention out the window. "Where are we?" she asked curiously.

"Just coming into Sedalia," Tony said, cracking his window a bit to allow some of the warm spring air to make its way into the car.

"Sedalia, Missouri. Isn't this where the state fair is held every year?" Libby asked curiously, looking out the car window with interest.

"Yes, the fairgrounds are just ahead. You ever been to the fair?"

"Once." Libby smiled softly at the memory. "It was a long time ago, but I can still remember the sounds, the smells. The laughter and the music from the calliope, the smell of grilling hot dogs and roasted peanuts. Ah, I love fairs." She laughed suddenly.

"What?" He smiled at her.

"I just remembered. Vinnie bought me a chameleon. Somehow they had managed to tie little chains around them with a safety pin so the poor little lizards could be worn on a blouse." Libby shook her head softly, memories flooding her. "I wore that chameleon every day for a week, each day with a different-colored blouse. I was utterly fascinated the way the chameleon changed colors." She looked at the deserted fairgrounds as they drove by. "It was a wonderful time," she added with another soft laugh. "Vinnie took me on every ride. He even managed to win me a funny-looking stuffed crocodile." She shook her head, remembering how much money her father had gone through in his efforts to win her the mangy-looking stuffed animal.

"It must have been difficult, raising a daughter single-handedly," he observed.

"Vinnie was a wonderful father. If I was a burden to him, he never showed it, and I never felt it. He's a very special man."

"But it must have been difficult for you at times, not having a mother."

Libby thought about it for a moment before she answered. "No, actually it wasn't. I was so young when she died. I don't remember her at all. I guess it's hard to miss something you never had."

"Sometimes mothers don't die...they just fade into the shadows."

Libby looked at him curiously, biting back the desire to ask him to elaborate on his strange statement. There was something about his tone of voice, the set of his shoulders that forbade her to question him. Apparently his light, flirtatious ways and his easy charm hid scars—deep ones that marked his soul. She repressed her need to reach out to him, to touch his arm, knowing he would hate her for a show of sympathy.

"You hungry?" he asked suddenly.

Libby shook her head. "No, but I could stretch my legs."

"My breakfast this morning was far too early to really count." He looked at his wristwatch and grinned. "And if we hurry, breakfast will be served for another ten minutes—I see the golden arches ahead. My stomach says it's time for a couple of egg biscuits and some hash browns." He pulled into the parking lot of the fast-food chain. "What about you?" he asked as they climbed out of the car.

"Just a cup of coffee," she said.

"I thought you said something about being a junk-food junkie."

She laughed. "I am, but I never indulge in my vices until after twelve noon."

One of his dark eyebrows shot up. "Vices? Hmm, as soon as I fill my stomach, I'd like to discuss the other vices you have besides eating junk food."

With a laugh, Libby gave him a small shove toward the order counter as she headed for the ladies' room.

Once in the rest room, she looked at her reflection in the mirror above the sink, dismayed at the tousled condition of her hair, the slight mascara smudges beneath her eyes. She washed her face with a wet paper towel, then finger-combed her hair as best she could. Better, she thought as she looked once again at her reflection. She didn't look half bad for a woman who was in the middle of a mystery that might possibly involve a breach of national security. "Oh, Vinnie, wait until you hear about this," she said softly, laughing as she tried to imagine her father's reaction.

By the time she left the rest room, Tony was nowhere to be seen. He must have gotten their order and gone back to the car. She left the brick building, raising her face to the warmth of the sun as she walked toward where Tony had parked. She frowned, startled as a car roared around the side of the building and squealed to a halt in front of her.

The passenger door burst open and before Libby had a chance to respond in any way, a pale, white-haired man jumped out and grabbed her arm. He roughly dragged her toward the open car.

The feel of his deathly cold hands on her arm broke the stunned inertia that had momentarily gripped her. She flailed out at the man, kicking and curving her fingers so her nails could be used as weapons. She didn't know what he wanted, or why he'd grabbed her, but she did know that if he got her into that car, she would be in the worst possible danger. She grunted in grim satisfaction as she raked her nails down the side of his face.

"You bitch," he grunted, his fetid breath smelling like death, his hands tightening their grip on her arm.

"Where is it?" he hissed through clenched teeth, his eyes suddenly lighting on the shimmering gold necklace almost hidden beneath her sweatshirt.

He growled in satisfaction and released his grip on her arm, instead grabbing the necklace in his large hand.

He yanked viciously, but the gold was thick and the clasp sturdy. The necklace clung to her neck possessively.

Her struggles shifted from trying to get away from the man, to grasping at the necklace, to keep herself from being strangled. As he grappled, pulling and tugging at the necklace, her air supply was slowly being cut off. *I'll strangle to death before it comes off,* she thought in panic, her vision beginning to blur. She choked, fighting back nausea as his unrelenting strength pulled the necklace tighter...tighter. She tried to kick out at him, but she was tiring, and his grip was maddeningly strong. She felt her eyes bulging, the cords of her neck taut as she pulled and gasped for blessed air. Tears squeezed from her eyes as her vision stopped blurring, but darkened ominously. Just as the darkness of unconsciousness threatened to claim her, she had an irrational burst of anger at Tony. He was apparently going to sit in his car and eat his damned breakfast, oblivious to the fact that she was dying.

Tony unwrapped his egg biscuit, his stomach rumbling with hunger as the scent of bacon and egg filled the interior of the car. As he took his first bite, a car squealed around the corner of the building, pulling up between his car and the front door of the place. Ah, another hungry morning traveler, he thought, finishing his biscuit in three big bites. He looked back toward the building, wondering what had happened to Libby. He was anxious to get back on the road, but he knew all about women and their secret rest room rituals. He'd never known a woman who could make a bathroom stop in under ten minutes.

He tilted his head to one side, strange sounds filtering

into his open window. A struggle... Yes, that's what it sounded like. He heard grunts, skin beating against skin...harsh noises that had no place in the beauty of the spring morning. His gaze shot back to the car parked between him and the building.

His nose twitched and the egg biscuit he'd just consumed turned to lead in the pit of his stomach. He jumped out of his car, simultaneously pulling his gun from the top of his boot. Rage ripped through him as he rounded the side of the car and saw Libby in a death grip. Her face was white and her eyes were opened wide, as if she saw her own death.

The man holding her looked up, startled at the sight of Tony with his gun drawn. "You son of a bitch," Tony snarled, his anger a force that vibrated around him. In an instant the man released Libby and jumped back into the car, which sped away with a shrill squeal of tires.

Tony didn't waste time chasing after the car or firing a shot after it. With his heart thudding painfully in his chest, he raced to where Libby lay pale and unmoving on the concrete of the parking lot. He shoved the gun back into the top of his boot as he crouched down next to her, his throat thick with emotion.

"Libby, are you all right?" He leaned down over her, moaning softly as he saw the red, angry welts around her slender, pale neck. He brushed a strand of her silky hair off her face, relief flooding through him as her eyelids fluttered rapidly, then opened.

"Remind me to buy you some nose spray," she uttered, her voice hoarse as he helped her struggle to a sitting position on the pavement.

"Nose spray?" He looked at her worriedly. Had she

hit her head on the pavement and now was suffering some sort of disorientation?

Libby nodded. "That famous nose of yours should have told you something like this was going to happen." She smiled weakly, then winced and rubbed her neck. "This peccadillo you have for eating breakfast is definitely dangerous to my well-being."

Tony smiled down at her in relief, touching the tip of her nose with the end of his finger. "Let's get the hell out of here," he said, gently helping her up and leading her to the car.

He eased her into the passenger seat of the car, his rage flaring again as he saw her unconsciously touch her neck and wince. His eyes narrowed as he thought of the man who had hurt her. Tony would kill him if given the chance.

"Did you get a good look at the men in the car?" Tony asked, maneuvering the lid off the cup of coffee and handing it to her.

Libby took the coffee gratefully, pausing a moment to take a sip of the hot brew, finding the heat soothing on her aching throat. "Not the driver, but I got a real good look at the man who grabbed me. He was white."

"You mean Caucasian," he corrected automatically, accustomed to years of taking down descriptions of suspects.

"No, I mean he was white...really white," Libby explained. "His skin was white, his hair was white and he had the eyes of a little mouse, all beady and pinkish." She shivered suddenly, realizing how close she had come to being strangled to death. Her skin still retained the evil cold clamminess of the man's hands and she shivered once again, never feeling more mortal than at this very moment.

"You mean he was an albino?" Tony asked, once again fighting a murderous rage as he felt the force of her shiver across the expanse of the front seat of the car.

"Yes...that's what he was...an albino...." Libby reached up and touched the gold of the necklace around her neck. How could anything so beautiful feel so evil... so frigid?

Tony reached over and took her hand. "Are you all right?"

She took a deep, steadying breath and smiled at him, finding his hand grasping hers comforting in a very nice way. "I'm fine." She smiled crookedly at him. "I'm a tough old bird."

As he wheeled the car back onto the highway, he released her hand, making her feel oddly bereft. She stared out the window, focused on the scenery, trying to regain a modicum of peace. Yes, she was a tough old bird, but she was being pushed to her limit. She reached up and touched the necklace once again. This was no game, and there were no civil rules of play.

"Damn," Tony muttered, checking his rearview mirror. "It looks like we've got company."

Libby whirled around, staring at the black sports car that quickly approached them. It was the same car that the albino had tried to pull her into. She checked her seat belt, making sure it was secure, her mouth suddenly dry as her stomach twisted in knots.

"Hang on...here they come," he said tersely, his knuckles white as he gripped the steering wheel.

The sports car slid alongside of Tony's car, metal crunching against metal as it swerved into the side of their car.

Libby stifled a scream. "What are they trying to do?" she gasped in horror.

"Force us off the road." He cursed as with another screech, the sports car slid into them again. Libby shoved the back of her hand into her mouth, trying to hold back another scream as Tony jerked the wheel sideways to escape.

"Hold on. I'm going to try to lose them." He punctuated his sentence by flooring the gas pedal, throwing Libby back against the seat with a burst of automotive power. Libby bit her bottom lip and braced herself with a hand against the dashboard, carefully juggling the cup of hot coffee in her other hand.

"We're going to have to get off this stretch of highway," Tony muttered, exploding with an expletive as a gunshot shattered their back windshield.

"Oh, God, they're shooting at us," Libby squeaked in terror.

Tony placed his hand on the top of her head and shoved her down on the seat next to him. "Keep your head down," he commanded. "I've got to get us off this highway. Right now we're sitting ducks for them."

Libby didn't need to be told twice to keep her head down. Her body strained against the confines of the seat belt, but she was barely aware of the cutting sensation. She crouched with her head against Tony's thigh, hardly conscious of the hot coffee that had splashed on her jeans. "I spilled my coffee," she remarked inanely, as the rest of the dark liquid quickly spread across the beige carpeting on the floor of the car.

"If we get out of this mess, you can pay for the car wash," Tony replied tersely as he suddenly wrenched the steering wheel to the right, causing the tires to squeal as he turned off the highway and onto a bumpy dirt road.

Libby's stomach did a series of erratic flip-flops, making her grateful she hadn't eaten anything. She squeezed her eyes tightly closed as she heard the resounding echo of more gunfire and Tony rounded another corner on what felt like two wheels. "Why do I suddenly get the feeling that I'm living out a scene from a 'Miami Vice' rerun?" she gasped, looking up at him from her crouched position on the seat.

"If you happen to see Don Johnson around, tell him we could use his help." Tony's jaw was clenched, his eyes narrowed to mere slits of concentration.

Libby closed her eyes once again as the car continued to travel bumpy back roads at bone-jarring high speed. She could hear the sound of tree branches swishing by and scratching the sides of the car as they flew over roads that were no more than cattle tracks.

As they zoomed over a particularly hard bump, Libby grasped Tony's thigh tightly. *We're going to die,* she thought, surprised that the thought brought with it no hysterical fear, only an intense anger because they were going to die and she wasn't sure why.

They would either have a wreck and die, or the men chasing them would catch them and kill them. She could envision Vinnie at her grave site, his grief deep and despairing. It wasn't fair...none of this was fair. She hadn't asked for any excitement in her life. She hadn't wanted an adventure.

"We've lost them." Tony's voice intruded into her morbid thoughts and she suddenly realized the car had slowed down.

"Are you sure?" she asked breathlessly, not moving from her position.

"I'm sure," he replied. "But I'm not sure what's worse, the claws on your cat or the claws on you."

His words made Libby realize that her fingers still dug into his thigh. "I'm sorry." She released her death grip on his thigh and sat up. "Like Twilight, I've also had all my shots."

He smiled at her, his eyes still radiating with dangerous glints. "Are you all right?" he asked tersely.

Libby shrugged and grinned jauntily. "Of course I'm fine. My pawnshop and apartment were vandalized. Some creep crept into my bedroom and put his filthy hand all over my mouth, a guy tried to strangle me in a McDonald's parking lot. I've got hot coffee burning a blister in my leg and I've just finished participating in a high-speed chase through the backwoods of the Ozarks. Heck, why shouldn't I be fine?" She realized she was on the verge of hysteria, but didn't know how to control it.

He pulled the car off into the thick growth at the side of the road, then shut off the engine. For a moment they both sat still, the interior of the car darkened by the thick brush that surrounded it. "Are you sure you're all right?" he asked, his dark eyes gazing at her intently.

"Yes, I'm fine," she replied tremulously, taking in a deep breath of air.

"Let me see that neck of yours." He turned in his seat and eyed her critically. Beneath the heavy gold necklace, the angry redness of her neck was already turning a vivid blue. "Damn them," he breathed, his fingers lightly caressing the smooth silkiness of the skin just above the bruised area. "Does it hurt much?" he asked, his dark gaze shining with anger, and something else…something that caused Libby's breath to come unevenly.

She shook her head, unsure whether her sudden breathlessness was a delayed reaction to her fear, or the result of the soft, gentle touch of his hand against the sensitive area of her throat.

"I promise you, nobody will get the chance to hurt you again. I'll kill them first," he promised and as he pulled her into the circle of his arms, she believed him.

But she didn't want to think about death. The scent of death had surrounded her for too long. The memory of the albino's cold hands on her arms had been like the fingers of death reaching out for her.

She wanted life. She wanted the feel of Tony's warm, vital body to chase away the last lingering vestiges of the graveyard. She needed to lose herself in his very aliveness.

As he swept a strand of her hair away from her face, she looked up at him. Gone was the anger in his eyes, replaced instead with a flame of fire that turned them into glowing chunks of charcoal. Without warning his lips took hers; hot and wet, they demanded a response. It was a demand she couldn't help but give in to.

She responded feverishly, clinging to him as if he were the only stable point in an all-too-dangerous world. His lips were hungry, aggressive, but no more than her own as she pressed against him, wanting to meld herself into the warmth and safety of his arms.

His lips devoured hers, his tongue invading and probing, and she welcomed him body and soul, allowing the flare of passion to take the place of her fear of death. She wanted the oblivion of his desire, the comfort of his warm, living body covering hers.

His hands slowly moved down the sides of her sweatshirt to the bottom, then just as slowly caressed upward inside the shirt, against the heat of her skin. She moaned deep in her throat as his hands cupped the mounds of her bra-covered breasts. His hands were fire and the icy fear of death left her as she reveled in being alive.

She ran her hands down his back, feeling the sinewy

muscles as she caressed downward, finally stopping to linger at his belt.

Her sweatshirt became an encumbrance to be rid of, and as he tugged at it, Libby helped him by raising her hands over her head and allowing the shirt to be pulled off and discarded into the back seat of the car.

She could smell him, dark and hungry, as his eyes lingered on her round full breasts, the nipples surging tightly against the lacy beige bra. "Libby..." His voice sounded tight as his thumbs brushed the top of the bra. He leaned down and placed his mouth against one peak. She could feel the heat of his lips through the thin material and suddenly she wanted the bra gone, swept away, so she could feel those lips against her flesh.

She reached around behind and unclasped the bra, shrugging her shoulders and allowing it to fall to her lap. The flame in his eyes burned brighter, threatening to consume her. "You're so beautiful," he breathed, his words ragged with his raspy breathing. He reached out and touched one of her nipples, catching and teasing it between thumb and index finger.

Libby felt her response beginning in the center of her stomach, a roiling heat and ache that slowly vibrated outward. She closed her eyes, emitting another small moan as his lips followed the path trailed by his fingers. She groaned as a nearly forgotten sensation of sexual splendor swept over her, intensifying the ache of need that throbbed in her lower stomach.

A thud on the roof of the car caused them both to burst apart.

A squirrel raced down the front windshield and disappeared into a nearby tree.

Tony expelled a deep breath as Libby released a shuddery sigh. He turned to reach for her again, but for

Libby, the spell was broken. "No, please..." she said, confused and embarrassed at the same time. "This...this is all crazy." She crossed her arms in front of her, shielding the sight of her naked breasts from his onyx eyes.

For a long moment they merely looked at each other. Libby could see her own confusion reflected in his eyes. With a muttered oath, he flung himself from the car and disappeared into the brush along the side of the road.

Libby watched him until he disappeared, then quickly scrambled for her sweatshirt in the back seat of the car. My God, where had her brain been? How had she allowed things to get so far out of control? She hardly knew the man, yet she'd been ready to... She shuddered as she thought of what they almost had done.

She pulled the shirt on over her head, then wrapped her arms around herself, the chill back in her veins. She'd encouraged what had just happened. She'd been afraid, off center, and had wanted his arms to wrap her up securely. But she hadn't considered what else she might promise in indulging her own needs.

She rubbed her forehead tiredly, overwhelmed by everything that had happened in such a short space of time. She couldn't process everything. Still, there was something about Tony Pandolinni that drew her to him. But she certainly hadn't intended to make love to him in the back seat of his car. She needed him to help her solve the mystery of the necklace. She needed his expertise in criminal matters—and that was *all* she needed.

She owed him an apology for allowing their physical intimacy to go as far as it had. She owed him an apology for unconsciously promising things her intellect wasn't prepared to give. Taking a deep, ragged breath, she leaned her head back against the car seat, gathering her thoughts before she went to find him and offer her apology.

Tony sat on a moss-covered rock, breathing deeply of the clean, country air, trying to eradicate the vision of Libby's bare breasts. It wasn't just the thought of her breasts that tormented him and made his desire difficult to kill. It was also the sound of her throaty moans, the sight of her passion-glazed azure eyes, the satiny feel of her heated flesh.

Damn it, he wanted her so badly, he ached with the need to take her, possess her, make her cry out his name in ecstasy.

He released a long, ragged sigh and clenched his trembling hands tightly together. He had been physically attracted to her from the moment he had first met her, but he'd been physically attracted to many women in the past, and never had he lost control as he had just now in the car. For heaven's sake, they had fallen on each other like sex-starved teenagers.

He breathed deeply once again, reflecting on all the times lately that he had come home after work and sat in his driveway, momentarily wishing there were somebody in the empty house waiting with a hot cup of coffee and a sympathetic shoulder.

Dangerous thinking, he admonished himself. He could always hire a housekeeper to make his coffee and a therapist to listen to all his problems. He didn't need a woman in his life. He'd been happy for thirty-six years without one. He wasn't about to compromise the vow he'd made long ago.

Still, even as he tried to dismiss thoughts of Libby, his mind filled with hazy, evocative images. Libby in her little blue teddy, handing him a freshly brewed cup of coffee, her eyes promising greater delights to come. Libby, lying in bed next to him, wrapping him up in her heat, enfolding him to her heart.

Fantasy, he chided himself angrily, unwilling to concede that there might be a need in him that Libby Weatherby, with her easy laughter and direct manner, might be able to fill.

He turned to see the object of his thoughts making her way through the thick underbrush toward him. She sat down next to him on the rock, and neither of them spoke for a long moment. Tony didn't want to talk to her, perversely irritated with her because she somehow made him feel vulnerable.

"Tony, I owe you an apology," she said softly, not looking at him but instead directing her attention out over the rolling hillside in the distance.

"You don't owe me anything," he countered tersely.

"On the contrary, I owe you for many things, but I definitely owe you an apology for that scene in the car," she said, coming right to the point with the straightforwardness he found both appealing and slightly unnerving. "I usually don't get myself into a position where I could be called a 'tease,' but that's exactly what I did, and for that I'm sorry."

When he didn't answer, she continued, "I really have no excuse for what happened...for letting things go so far. I guess I was scared and I suddenly realized how mortal we are and well, I guess it's the same way a lot of people felt during World War II. I suppose there were a lot of babies conceived in bomb shelters. I think I read about that sort of thing someplace—it's some sort of phenomenon...people reaching out for passion in times of facing death—" She broke off and looked at him.

As she talked, Tony felt his anger dissipating. After

all, her explanation made his whole crazy feelings for her—the whole crazy scene in the car—make a certain kind of sense. Of course, they had both responded to the stress of being chased, the fear of being hurt or killed. It was a sort of war-induced sexual freedom. They had smelled death and destruction and had responded by reaching out for each other in the oldest form of communication in the world. It had nothing to do with any special feelings for her; it had nothing to do with her at all. He would have reacted the same to any woman in the same circumstances.

He turned and smiled at her, feeling relieved. "Making love in a crowded bomb shelter has got to be easier than making love in the front seat of a car...especially with dancing squirrels in the area."

She returned his smile, obvious relief on her face, as well. "I think we both agree that what happened between us in the car was a crazy mistake. We've been thrown together due to a bizarre twist of fate, and we shouldn't let that fact force us into a personal relationship we might regret." She looked at him, her blue eyes serious and level. "I think the best way for us to handle this is to work as business partners, with no personal entanglements to muddle things up."

"Absolutely," Tony agreed instantly, relieved that their relationship had not only been identified in words, but agreed upon, as well.

"Partners?" She thrust her hand out to him.

He hesitated only a moment. "Partners," he agreed, taking her small hand in a firm handshake, ignoring the way even the mere physical contact of her hand in his caused tingles of pleasure to dance up his arm. "We'd better get back on the road," he said, releasing her hand.

She nodded.

As they walked back to the car, Tony was pleased that apparently she wasn't looking for a relationship, either. It made things so much less complicated, and they had enough complications just trying to keep one step ahead of the men who were after them.

Now, if he could just forget the hot, sweet taste of her mouth against his. If he could just forget the feel of her silky flesh, the way her breasts had swelled, as if in anticipation of his caress....

A lapse of memory would certainly make things easier, he thought as he started up the car. But one thing Tony had learned through the years was that life was rarely easy.

Chapter 7

"How far are we from Dr. Higgens's lab?" Libby asked once they were traveling again on the narrow dirt road.

"I'm not sure," Tony replied thoughtfully. "If I knew where we were, I'd know how far it was to the lab."

"Are you telling me we're lost?" Libby stared at him in dismay.

"Well, I wasn't exactly noticing street signs while we were trying to escape our pursuers," he replied dryly. "Besides," he continued, smiling at her confidently, "I'm sure we're just a mile or so off the main highway."

As the minutes turned into hours and still they couldn't find the main road, Tony was grateful for one thing: Libby didn't say a word. She didn't chastise him, she didn't lose patience and he got no feeling of censure from her silence.

Libby was too busy enjoying the beautiful scenery to notice the passing of time. Even though she was anxious to find Jasper Higgens's lab and discover some answers as to the value of the golden necklace around her neck, she'd never been this far into the hills of the Ozarks. She looked out the window of the car with interest.

The rolling hills were covered with spring-awakened wildflowers, and the car passed by dozens of springs and creeks of sparkling clean water. Not only was there a profusion of beautiful plants and flowers, but the area was rife with wildlife. Several times Tony managed to swerve across the gravel road to avoid hitting a hopping rabbit, and once they had rounded a corner and caught sight of a startled deer disappearing farther into the woods along the side of the road.

"Do you think we need to worry about those men finding us again?" she asked, unconsciously raising her hand to touch the bruised area round her neck.

Tony shook his head. "If we don't know where we are, I don't see how they'll be able to find us." He sighed tiredly. "The problem I'm having is that most of these roads around here are just farm trails, with no markings, no street signs to let me get my bearings."

Libby could hear the exhaustion in his voice and noticed that the lines in his face had deepened with the passing of hours. She had slept earlier in the car, but she knew he was functioning on the scant sleep of the night before. "Tony, why don't you pull the car off to the side of the road and take a little nap," she suggested. "At this point, an hour or two one way or the other isn't going to make much difference as to when we get to the lab and you have to be completely exhausted."

"I am tired," he admitted. "It's been about a week since I got a really good night's sleep."

"You look tired," she said, fighting the impulse to

reach out and stroke his brow. "Surely an hour nap will make us both feel better."

"Okay," he said reluctantly. "I guess a short stop won't hurt anything." He drove a few more minutes, then found an area where they could pull far enough off the road so the car wasn't visible. "We should be okay here," he said, shutting off the engine.

"Why don't you get into the back seat. You'd have more room to stretch out back there," she suggested, knowing she could fit her small frame in the front seat and not be hindered by the steering wheel and column.

Tony nodded. He climbed out of the car and got into the back seat, folding himself awkwardly to find a position of comfort in the small confines of the area. Within seconds he was breathing deeply and regularly, sound asleep.

Libby peeked over the top of the front seat, studying him, feeling slightly guilty, as if she were intruding on a private moment by watching him sleep. Yet she was unable to stop herself from taking the opportunity to look at him without his dark eyes returning the gaze.

She crossed her arms on the back of the seat and rested her chin there, drinking her fill of the man in the back seat. He looked younger, more vulnerable with the lines of tension on his face eased and his mouth slightly open.

She'd seen the hard edge of danger on his features, she'd marveled at the fires of passion in his eyes and now she eyed him covetously, noting the dark stubble that had begun to appear on his cheeks and chin, the furrow between his dark brows that even in sleep didn't totally disappear. His smile was magnetic, charming in its openness. It was only when one looked into his eyes that they realized the smile didn't quite reach that deep.

She noted the firm planes of his stomach where his T-shirt had ridden up slightly. There wasn't a spare inch of fat on him, but that didn't mean he was thin. He was rip-cord lean but possessed a wiry strength and broad shoulders. Her gaze went farther down his body, noting how the tight jeans hugged his flesh, emphasizing his muscular thighs.

She closed her eyes, remembering the heat of his kiss, the hunger that had coiled up in her stomach like a king cobra snake. He'd stoked a flame in her that hadn't been tended to in a long time. She hadn't thought about sex since her divorce, had rarely thought about it in the last year of her marriage. With Bill, lovemaking had always been on his terms, when he felt the need. It had been quick and emotionless. But Tony made her think of sex…wild, abandoned, uninhibited sex that lasted for hours. He made her think of hot, sultry nights, equally hot hands caressing her skin and peaks of pleasure reached again and again.

She mentally shook herself. These kinds of thoughts were counterproductive. She had a feeling Tony Pandolinni had some heavy emotional baggage. He definitely wasn't a good bet for happily-ever-after. And she wasn't the type to indulge in a good old-fashioned bout of lovemaking just for the physical pleasure that could be achieved. She was a happily-ever-after kind of woman. And at the moment she had more important things on her mind than making love with Tony Pandolinni.

Feeling restless and not wanting to bother Tony's much-needed sleep, Libby quietly opened the car door and slipped into the warm spring sunshine. She stood next to the car and stretched languidly, feeling her muscles uncramp from the long hours in the car.

She looked around with interest, enjoying the beauty of the surrounding countryside. In the distance she could hear what sounded like the faint trickling of a stream. She followed the sound, stepping carefully through the thick underbrush that lined the side of the road. She made her way slowly, pushing aside the high weeds and thornbushes that attempted to grab and scratch at her as she made her way toward the sound of the water. The scent of spring surrounded her, the smell of flowers and greenery.

About fifty feet from the road, she broke into a small clearing and caught her breath as she saw a small stream of brilliant blue, sparkling water. Oh, the beauty of this area... She felt like an explorer, the first human being ever to find this particular stream.

She spotted a large rock jutting out at the edge of the water and carefully made her way to it. Perching precariously atop it, she looked around and took a deep breath, tilting her head upward to the afternoon sunshine.

Oh, it would be so easy to forget everything that had happened to her in the past two days. It would be so easy to fall into a false sense of security.

Sitting here on the mossy rock, smelling the scent of the wildflowers and clean spring water, it would be easy to dismiss the events of the past couple of days as nothing more than the horrendous lingering memories of a nightmare.

She reached up and touched her neck beneath the heavy gold necklace. But nightmares didn't produce welts and bruises. She frowned, remembering the shattered items in her pawnshop, the total disrespect for the things in her apartment. Damn those people, whoever they were. Damn them for their vicious attacks on her. Where before, she might have handed them the necklace and washed her hands of the whole mess, now she'd be damned before they would get their hands on what they wanted.

She fumbled with the latch on the necklace, finally unlatching the clasp, allowing it to fall into her hand. It was a beautiful piece. The minute she had seen it, she'd known she would give the man whatever he wanted for it. The craftsmanship of the piece was exquisite. The delicate locket in the center was attached to meshlike gold.

She clutched it tightly in her hands, thinking of the little old man who'd brought it in. Jasper Higgens had reminded her of a little elf...diminutive, with big ears and gray hair. It was difficult to believe that he was now dead.

She squeezed the necklace even tighter. She could fling it into the woods. Chances were nobody would ever find it again. Or she could bury it deep in the rich earth and nobody would ever see it again. But even as these thoughts crossed her mind, she dismissed them. She was intrigued and wanted to know what secret the necklace held...a secret that had already cost a man his life.

She wasn't a quitter. The harder she was pushed, the more she'd push back. Of course, it was nice to know she wasn't in this mess all alone. Tony was turning out to be something of a guardian angel. If he hadn't come to her aid in the parking lot, she had a feeling the albino would have strangled her to death.

Tony... Again, thoughts of the man brought a rush of strange heat to her stomach. It was obvious there was some sort of sexual attraction between them, but as long as that could be held in check, their partnership was comfortable. It was possible they could come out of this as good friends, and this thought was certainly not unpleasant. The one thing Libby had missed most since her divorce was male companionship. Being raised by her father, she'd always been comfortable in the company of males.

With this pleasant thought in mind, she placed the necklace back around her neck, closed her eyes and scooted into a more comfortable position on the rock.

Tony awoke suddenly, an emptiness gnawing in the pit of his stomach. For a moment he was disoriented as to where he was. He looked around without moving, tense and ready for anything. Then he remembered. He was in the back seat of his car. He sat up, fully expecting to see Libby sound asleep in the front seat.

His heart gave an erratic thud as he looked over the seat and saw nothing there. He quickly scanned the immediate area outside of the car, feeling his heartbeats increase when there was no sign of Libby.

Where was she? Surely he hadn't slept so soundly that he wouldn't have heard if somebody had found them and taken her. His heart nearly exploded out of his chest as he thought about the scene in the parking lot at the fast-food place. Surely he would have heard something…a struggle of some sort…wouldn't he?

He stumbled out of the back seat, his stomach muscles clenching tightly. He pulled his small pistol from the top of his boot and walked several steps away from the car. "Libby?" he called, his voice taut with tension. He felt sick to his stomach when there was no answer. Where was she? Had something happened? God, he'd never forgive himself if something happened to her. He gripped his gun painfully tight, his whole body vibrant with energy. "Libby, where the hell are you?"

"Hi. Did you have a good nap?" She stepped out of

the underbrush right next to Tony, smiling brightly. Her smile faded as she saw the gun leveled at her chest.

"Damn it, Libby, you almost got yourself shot!" he exploded, uncocking the gun and shoving it back into the top of his boot.

His utter relief at seeing her safe and unharmed gave way to irrational anger. "Don't you ever do that again." He grabbed her by the shoulders and gave her a small shake. "Don't you ever leave and not tell me where you're going. And don't you ever sneak up on me like that."

He glared at her, his anger suddenly spent as he saw the bewilderment in her vivid blue eyes. "I'm sorry." He released his grip on her and stepped back, running a hand through his dark hair in distraction. "I woke up and you weren't anywhere to be seen, and I thought..."

"No, I'm sorry." She reached out and touched his arm lightly, her blue eyes contrite and huge. "I didn't even think about you being worried if you woke up and found me gone. It was very thoughtless of me."

The last of Tony's anger left him as he gazed at her. She was so different from any woman he'd ever known—so ready to admit fault if fault was hers. He knew she would be just as quick to demand an apology should the fault not be hers.

"It's all right. I overreacted, and yes, I had a good nap." He looked at his watch, surprised to see that he had slept for a little over two hours. "We'd better get moving. We've lost a great deal of time today."

An hour later they drove into the first town they had seen since leaving Sedalia so many hours earlier. Cob Corners was actually not even much of a town, boasting only a general store, a filling station and a small engine-repair shop.

"I'll get some directions here," Tony said, pulling into the gas station. "I also need to make a few phone calls." He hoped a call to Cliff would provide some information about the men who were after them.

Libby nodded. "I think I'll check and see if they have any interesting soda or vending machines."

"Ah, looking for junk food?" he asked with a grin.

"You know it. A couple of candy bars and a can of soda and I'll feel fresh as a daisy."

"Did you folks pull in here for some gas, or just to find a place to jaw with each other?" a gruff voice asked from outside Tony's car window.

They both looked to see an old man clad in faded overalls. His faded blue eyes gazed at them curiously.

"You can fill it up with unleaded," Tony told the man as he got out of the car. "Do you have a pay phone inside?"

"Yup," he answered, and began to fill up the car as Libby and Tony went inside the station.

"Evening, folks." A plump woman with brilliant pink cheeks and curly gray hair sat behind the cash register in the dimly lit interior of the station.

"Good evening," Tony responded. "The man outside said there was a pay phone in here." He smiled his thanks as the woman pointed to a phone on a wall.

"Beautiful evening, isn't it?" the woman said with friendliness as Libby perused the contents of an antiquated vending machine.

"Beautiful," Libby agreed with a smile, making her decision and feeding in the proper coins.

"Yes, sir, I suppose a pretty spring day like this makes everyone want to get out and take a drive," the woman continued chattering as Libby made another selection. "We've had more business this afternoon than we've had in a month of Sundays. We had a nice family stop in right after noon. Out for a drive, they were, but the kids had to use the rest room.'' The woman grinned, showing several spaces where teeth had once been. ''You know how little tykes are, bladders no bigger than peanuts.''

Libby murmured something appropriate and fed in the last of her coins as the woman continued. ''But some folks we get passing through here, they aren't worth God's spit. Like those two who were here a while ago...one dark as the devil himself and the other pale like a ghost.''

Libby's heart dropped to her feet at the woman's innocent words. She turned away from the machine and stared at the woman. ''The pale man...he was an albino?'' she asked breathlessly.

''Yes.'' The woman's eyes narrowed and she looked at Libby suspiciously. ''Friends of yours?'' Gone was the aura of country friendliness from the old woman.

''On the contrary,'' Libby murmured, a chill dancing up and down her spine. ''We...uh...encountered them on the road some time ago and they nearly caused us to have an accident,'' she improvised, grabbing her snacks from the vending machine.

The woman clucked her tongue sympathetically, friendliness back in her twinkling eyes. ''Some days I just wonder what the good Lord was thinking about when he put men like that on this earth.''

Libby nodded and smiled absently, her eyes searching for Tony, who was still talking in low murmurs on the phone across the room. ''S'cuse me,'' she said to the woman and hurried over to Tony. ''Tony...'' The urgency of her voice made him turn and look at her immediately. ''They were here...the albino and his friend in the sports car. They were here just a while ago. They must still be looking for us.''

"Cliff, I'll call you later tonight," Tony said into the phone. "I need anything and everything you can find out. I'll get back to you later." Tony hung up the phone and put an arm around Libby's trembling shoulders. "Come on, let's get out of here."

Moments later they were driving again, this time with directions from the attendant who had filled up their gas tank. "Damn, I hate functioning in the dark," Tony muttered, his eyes constantly checking his rearview mirror as he drove. "If we knew exactly what value that necklace had, we'd know which authorities to hand it over to, but until we know what it represents, I can't just give it to anyone. CIA men can be bought just as easily as anyone else," Tony said. "You have no idea how many double agents there are in the agency."

"Surely there's one honest, patriotic man working for the CIA," Libby countered, equally impatient.

"Give me his name and I'll be glad to hand the necklace to him," Tony stated emphatically.

Libby hugged her displeasure. "You are a cynic," she exclaimed. "Working for the police department for so many years has made you perceive everyone as an enemy."

"And you are naive," Tony returned. "Working in the confines of a neighborhood pawnshop amid your antiques and treasures has made you see everything through a rose-tinted veil. Haven't you heard, spying is big business.... Ask Mrs. Walker."

"Who's Mrs. Walker?" she asked curiously.

Tony rolled his eyes in exasperation. "The Walker case was only one of the most well-publicized cases of spying this country has seen."

"Well, excuse my ignorance," Libby said stiffly. "Had I known I was going to get caught up in the middle of a national security crisis I would have taken a class in how to evade spies and protect national secrets." She glared at him, suddenly angry at him for making her feel stupid. She was not having a red-letter day, and his condescending attitude was the last straw.

"It would have been helpful if you had read a book or taken a class in picking an agency man you can trust," Tony exclaimed, his mustache twitching with amusement.

"Or taken notes the last time I went to see a James Bond movie," she replied, her anger dissipating as she recognized the completely ludicrous nature of their argument.

"Or at least watched reruns of 'Get Smart,'" Tony said with a wide grin.

"That's definitely more in my league." Libby giggled, taking off her shoe and holding it up to her ear like a telephone. "Hello, Control. Could you tell me again, who are the bad guys?"

Suddenly they were both laughing. Uproarious laughter that fed upon itself. Libby recognized the laughter for exactly what it was, a release of the tension they'd felt since leaving Kansas City and encountering so many problems. Yet, even realizing this, she allowed the laughter to overtake her. As she wiped at the tears in her eyes and held her aching sides, she realized this was the first time she'd heard Tony really laugh. He had a pleasant one, a low, full rumble that caused a funny sensation in the pit of her stomach. The sound of his laughter was one she would like to hear more often.

It was Tony who sobered first, the light slowly fading from his dark eyes. "Libby, I think it's obvious these

men know where we're going. They know about the lab
and they've guessed that's where we're headed." He
paused a moment, then continued. "I think maybe it
would be a good idea for us to hole up for a day or two.
Maybe if we don't turn up at the lab today or tomorrow,
those goons will think we turned around and headed
back to Kansas City."

"You really believe that?" she asked dubiously,
rather uncomfortable at the idea of sharing a motel room
with him, yet even more uncomfortable at the thought
of being in a room alone or at the mercy of the man
with the deathlike eyes.

Tony shrugged. "I don't know what to believe. I do
know those men are anticipating our moves, so perhaps
it's time we change the game. By holing up for a day
or two, maybe we can throw them off the track."

"Whatever you think is best is fine with me," she
said, then frowned worriedly.

"What's wrong?" Tony asked.

"Twilight. I assumed we'd be back at your place late
tonight, and I didn't leave much food out for him."

"He can always feast on the remainder of my flesh,
which is probably still under his claws," he joked, then
continued. "If it will make you feel better, when we stop
for the night I'll call my neighbors and see that they
feed the beast. They often take care of things for me
when I'm out of town or on a case."

"I'd appreciate it," she said gratefully.

"I'm starving," Tony said suddenly. "That's two
things I have against those goons. First, they fired bullets
at me, which always puts me in a foul mood. And secondly, they made me throw down my biscuit this morning. And they've had us running so crazy this afternoon,
we haven't even had time for lunch."

Libby grinned and pulled the goodies she had purchased at the gas station from the glove compartment. "Food," she announced.

"What have you got?" Tony asked eagerly.

"Gummi Bears, peanut-butter cups and M&M's."

Tony groaned. "That isn't food," he protested.

"Mmm, it's ambrosia," she exclaimed, ripping open the Gummi Bears and popping a red one into her mouth. "What is your pleasure?" she asked.

"My pleasure would be a juicy steak and a baked potato, but I guess I'll take a peanut-butter cup. However, the first decent restaurant we see, we're stopping. Maybe you can be happy with little bears and chocolate, but I need a real meal."

Libby laughed and popped another candy into her mouth.

It was nearly an hour later when they pulled into a town large enough to have not only a café but a motel of sorts, as well. The town was called Muddy Creek, and the sign outside of town said it had been established in 1824.

The motel was the Muddy Creek Motel and boasted ten little housekeeping cabins. "It's not exactly high class, is it?" Tony asked, obviously dismayed by the ramshackle appearance of the place.

Libby eyed the unpainted, ill-kempt buildings. Surrounded by overgrowth and tangled vines, they didn't exactly radiate welcome. She swallowed her dismay. "As long as they have beds and a good hot shower, they'll be all right for a night or two."

"At least it's off the beaten track."

She nodded, knowing they'd traveled almost twenty minutes off the main road to find the out-of-the-way town. Surely they'd be safe here. Surely those men wouldn't be able to find them. She looked at the forlorn buildings. "If the owner looks like Anthony Perkins, we're finding another motel," she said, scenes of an old horror movie playing in her head.

"It's a deal." Tony laughed as he got out of the car.

She waited in the car while Tony went into the office and took care of the necessary paperwork. While he was gone, she looked around again, wondering how the motel managed to survive in this remote area.

"I asked them for the cabin farthest from the office," he explained as he joined her back in the car. He grinned at her sheepishly. "I told them we were newlyweds and didn't want to be disturbed or disturb anyone else. I figure if we are in the farthest cabin, we can park the car where it can't be seen from the road."

"Did you get a double?" she asked. "You know, a room with two beds," she continued as he looked at her in confusion.

"Libby, that would have been rather suspect. First, I tell them we're newlyweds, then I ask for a room with two beds?"

"Oh, of course. I wasn't thinking," she said, feeling a hot flush sweep over her face as she thought of sharing the same bed with Tony. "It really doesn't matter. I mean, we're both rational adults."

"Certainly," he agreed confidently. "If you're worried about that scene in the car earlier this morning, I think we both agree that was nothing more than a reaction of sorts to the stress of the situation. Isn't that right?"

"Oh, yes," she readily agreed. "It was just a fluke, a momentary lapse of sanity."

"But, of course, if you're worried that you might lose control once again..." A twinkle glittered in his eyes.

"Don't be ridiculous," Libby snapped. But there was something about the idea of sharing a motel room with Tony Pandolinni that made her sense danger...a danger that was strangely evocative...and extremely appealing.

Chapter 8

"Let's go get something to eat," Tony suggested. "I
saw a little restaurant down the road a ways and I don't
know about you, but I'm starving."

"Sounds good to me," Libby agreed, still contemplating the night and the sleeping arrangements to come.

They looked at each other dubiously as a sullen waitress led them to a table in the back of the Muddy Creek
Restaurant. The room was dark and dank and smelled of
old age and mildew.

"If the food is as good as the atmosphere, we may
not have to worry about those goons finding us," Tony
said as the waitress departed with their orders.

"Why is that?" Libby asked, swatting at a lazy fly
that buzzed irritatingly around her head.

"Because we'll die of ptomaine poisoning long before
the night is over." He smiled at her ruefully.

Libby laughed, but then her grin slowly left her face

and she looked at him reflectively. "You know this afternoon, while you were sleeping in the car...?"

Tony nodded. "What about it?"

"I found this beautiful spring creek with a big rock jutting out in the water. I sat on the rock for a long time, contemplating throwing the necklace into the water or burying it in a hole." She reached up and touched the necklace, fingering the locket in the center. "I figured, why not? Nobody would know where it was. It would probably never be found again."

"So why didn't you?" Tony asked softly.

"That was the problem...that nobody would know where it was. Just because I threw the necklace into the water, that wouldn't stop those men from chasing us. And what would happen if they caught me and I didn't have it anymore—if I told them I threw it away?" She shivered at the very thought. She had a feeling the albino's rage would be a horrendous sight to behold. "Anyway, I decided if I get rid of the necklace, it has to be in a way those men will know with a certainty that I no longer have it." She shrugged and smiled at him, raising her chin a fraction of an inch. "Besides, they've made me mad, and I'm intrigued. I want to know what it is about this necklace that's worth so much excitement."

Tony smiled at her in open admiration. "You're one hell of a woman, Libby Weatherby. Most women who found themselves in your shoes would find a hole to crawl into and never come out."

"I have a feeling these particular men would find whatever hole I was in and drag me out by my hair," she said, ignoring the warmth of pleasure that coursed through her at his compliment.

This is ridiculous, she scoffed to herself. Why should

she care if Tony Pandolinni thought she was a special kind of woman? All she wanted from him was his expertise in eluding the men who chased them and getting the necklace into the right hands.

"What are we going to do if we get to this lab and we can't find anyone who has any answers?" she asked, refusing to dwell on the strange warmth his words had evoked inside her.

"I'm hoping that won't happen," he replied thoughtfully. "I'm hoping Jasper Higgens had friends, associates, somebody who was close enough to him to have some answers. But if he didn't, I'm hoping we can get a lead through the sports car and the men chasing us. I got the license number, and I'm hoping that Cliff can tell me exactly who they are. That information might bring some additional answers."

Libby nodded and they both fell silent as the waitress appeared with their orders.

Surprisingly enough, the food was excellent. Tony's steak was thick and juicy, cooked perfectly to his requested medium rare. Libby's hamburger was nearly platter-size, loaded with the works. The French fries were the thick, home-style kind, fried to a deep, golden brown.

Conversation ceased as they devoured the food in front of them. Even though Tony gave the aura of being relaxed, Libby noticed his gaze shot to the door of the restaurant each time it opened. Libby knew it bothered him that the men in the sports car were close by. It bothered her, too. She wondered if she would ever be able to forget the feel of the albino's cold hands around her throat, the look of death that had radiated from his eyes.

She shook her head, refocusing her attention on the

food. Who knew when they would get a good meal again in the next day or two?

It was some time later when Tony shoved his plate away and looked across the table at Libby. "When you're finished, we'll go back to the motel room and I'll make a couple of phone calls."

"I'm finished," Libby replied, also pushing her plate away with a contented sigh. "I can't remember when I ate that much in a single sitting."

"It's been a long day," Tony said with a smile.

"Ah, the master of the understatement," Libby replied dryly, a small smile lifting one corner of her mouth. "It's definitely a day I won't forget for a long time to come."

They left the restaurant and made one stop before going to their motel room. Libby spotted a tiny general store and asked Tony to stop so she could pick up a few toiletries. Within minutes she was back in the car with a large brown bag.

Tony parked the car in the wooded area at the side of the small dilapidated cabin. "I can't believe we paid good money for this place," Tony complained as they went inside. He wrinkled his nose at the musty scent that greeted them. "At least it looks clean," he added grudgingly.

Libby nodded, surprised to find it so. The antiquated stove and refrigerator on the other side of the room gleamed with cleanliness and no dust lay on the cigarette-scarred dresser. The gold bedspread was partially turned down on the double bed, revealing pristine white sheets.

"Once the windows are opened a bit, maybe the smell won't be so bad," Tony said, opening one of the small windows in the front of the cabin.

"I don't mind the smell," Libby replied, setting her paper bag of toiletries on the cheap-looking kitchen table. "In fact, it sort of reminds me of the smell in the pawnshop. It's the scent of old furniture, history, people's lives," she finished, suddenly feeling awkward. Other than the kitchen table and the dresser, the only other piece of furniture in the room was the double bed, which looked incredibly small. "I...I think I'll just go take a shower," she murmured, feeling her face flushing heatedly. She picked up her sack of things and disappeared into the bathroom.

Tony breathed a sigh of relief when she was gone. He had sensed her sudden awkwardness and had responded with one of his own. God, it had been years since he had been in a motel room with an attractive woman. In fact, the last time had been when he'd been in college.

He smiled at the sudden memory. In those days there had been no such thing as coed dorms. His girlfriend of the moment had snuck out of her sorority house on a forged overnight pass and he had rented a motel room much like this one. What should have been a romantic, exciting tryst had instead ended in a heated argument. His girlfriend had been angry that he'd brought her to such a seedy place, ignoring the fact that he was a struggling student with very little money to spend. The night had ended in frustration, and there had been no lovemaking.

"And this night will be the same," he said softly aloud, irritated when he recognized a certain wistfulness in his voice.

Damn, Libby was definitely getting under his skin. Libby and her big, azure eyes that did nothing to hide her feelings. She was so damned honest, so up-front—and yet so vulnerable. He was beginning to like her, and that was what scared the hell out of him. He could handle pure lust, a total sexual attraction, but he wasn't so sure of the new feelings that he was experiencing.

He expelled a groan of confusion and aggravation and sat down on the edge of the bed. He reached for the phone and punched in the long-distance numbers that would connect him with his friend at the police department back in Kansas City.

"Marchelli," the voice said on the other end of the line.

"Cliff, it's Tony. Do you have anything for me?"

"Do I? Tony, where the hell are you?" Cliff asked worriedly. "I've been trying to get in touch with you all day."

"I'm in a little town called Muddy Creek, someplace deep in the Ozarks area."

"What in the hell are you doing down there, and why did you want to know about those men?" Cliff demanded. "Damn it, Tony, are you involved with the Higgens murder case? I told you we'd been pulled off that case and the red flag is out for the local authorities to keep their noses out of it."

"I can't do that," Tony answered firmly. "My nose has been put out of joint with this."

"Your butt is going to be burned if you don't back off and get in touch with the chief. You may have quit the department, but the chief wants to know exactly what you're doing in the middle of all this."

"Tell him I'm on vacation," Tony replied. "Just tell him I'm in a motel room with a beautiful blonde and I'll be back in town in a couple of days."

"Yeah, right," Cliff said dryly. "And while I'm at it, I'll tell him you and this fictional blonde were kidnapped by a UFO and last seen flying over Omaha." Cliff sighed impatiently. "Come on, Tony, be straight and tell me what's going on."

"I can't right now, because I don't know," Tony admitted. "Tell me what you got off the license number I gave you."

"The car is registered to one Richard D. Hawkins, and Mr. Hawkins is not exactly a model citizen. I pulled everything I could on him, and the man has a record a mile long, everything from arson and armed robbery to conspiracy to commit murder. Unfortunately, the man has a lot of money behind him and hasn't spent more than two years at a time in prison. Seems he's fallen out of sight recently, and he's suspected of being affiliated with an underground organization called the New Republic of Man. This organization is another offbeat supremacist group that is looking for an opportunity to rule the world. The one thing that makes this different from all the other cults and kooks is that the New Republic seems to be extremely well organized and well financed. These are not your ordinary nut cases." Cliff paused to take a breath.

"What about known associates?" Tony asked, thoughtfully digesting all that Cliff had been able to find out. Thank God Cliff was conscientious. Tony knew he'd gone to a lot of trouble to find out everything he'd told him so far.

"One William Radford Taylor, an albino. Tony, this is one bad dude," Cliff exclaimed. "He's a known mercenary, trained in every lethal art there is, and he is a sociopath with no conscience, no ethics, no loyalty. Whatever you've become involved in, Tony, you're in way over your head." He exploded once again. "Damn it, Tony, you aren't exactly Rambo."

"Thanks for your vote of confidence, partner," Tony

replied dryly, then continued. "You don't happen to know anyone trustworthy in the CIA, do you?"

Cliff expelled another breath of colorful language. "I don't know what you've gone and gotten yourself involved in, but you'd better get yourself uninvolved real quick. These men are not two-bit hoods—they're professionals and they're deadly."

"If I could get myself uninvolved, I would. I'm no hero," Tony said truthfully. "But, Cliff, there really is a beautiful blonde involved."

"Yeah, and my mother was a centerfold for *Playboy* last month," Cliff remarked with a snort, then sighed with resignation. "If I can't talk you into coming back and dropping this whole thing, the least you can do is keep in constant touch and call for reinforcements if you need them. Will you at least do that much?"

"You've got a deal," Tony agreed. "And one last thing.... Did you happen to read or learn anything about Jasper Higgens's associates or assistants before you were pulled off the case?"

"Yeah, come to think of it, I do remember seeing something about a Jonathon Maxwell. He was a lab assistant with Higgens. I think they were getting ready to run a check on him before we got pulled off."

"Great. Thanks a lot, Cliff," Tony said.

"Tony, be careful," Cliff said, as Tony slowly hung up the phone.

Libby stood beneath the spray of water, grateful that the shower was wonderfully warm and the spray was full and relaxing. She felt as if she'd accumulated a full week's worth of grime in this single day. She scrubbed at her arms, trying to banish the remembered feel of the albino's hands on her.

She lathered her hair, liberally using the shampoo she'd bought in the general store.

In fact, the general store had been heaven-sent in making an unexpected night in a motel room more pleasant. Not only had she purchased shampoo, but also toothbrushes and paste, two T-shirts and several other items. At least she and Tony wouldn't have to sleep in the same clothes they had worn all day.

She flushed at the thought of sharing the same bed with him all night long. She lowered the temperature of the hot water, suddenly finding it a little too warm.

Somehow, someway, Tony Pandolinni had crept beneath her defenses. She'd thought she wanted to remain alone, a divorced woman rediscovering her independence. But suddenly she was beginning to realize there was a difference between being independent and being alone. She'd liked being married, liked sharing her life with somebody special. She missed having that special connection. Yes, in the months since her divorce, she'd been independent, but she'd also been lonely.

Tony was so unlike Bill. From the first day of their marriage, Bill had set about to destroy Libby's sense of independence, forced her to be a mere reflection of what he wanted and demanded. She had a feeling Tony would want a woman who knew her own mind, who strove to maintain her own identity. And therein lay the danger...

She stepped beneath the stinging spray of water to rinse the shampoo from her hair and banish any thoughts of a relationship with Tony from her head.

She had a feeling that a relationship with Tony would only lead to heartache. He gave his charm easily, he'd give physical pleasure, but he would never, ever, give his heart. In that respect, she had a feeling Tony Pandolinni was a horribly stingy man.

Yes, she'd be a fool to allow anything to happen between she and Tony, and Vinnie hadn't raised a fool. Smiling confidently, she turned off the water and stepped out of the shower.

Tony looked up as the bathroom door opened and Libby stepped out. Immediately the room filled with the fresh, clean scent of the soap and shampoo she had used. Tony's chest suddenly ached as his breath became caught someplace between his ribs. God, she looked so clean and fresh, so beautiful. She was clad only in a huge T-shirt that fell almost to her knees. She didn't seem aware of the fact that the cotton material clung to her rounded breasts and emphasized rather than hid the darker circles of her nipples. Her face had the clean, scrubbed beauty of good health, and her pale hair was drying in a fluffy cloud of softness.

"Did you get your phone calls made?" she asked, sitting down primly at the small kitchen table.

He nodded slowly, hoping the tumultuous emotions he felt weren't reflected on his face.

"What did you find out?" She leaned forward eagerly, the top of the T-shirt falling away from her body, exposing her delicate collarbone.

"Uh...we'll talk about it after I shower," he murmured, jumping off the bed and disappearing into the bathroom.

"There's a bottle of shampoo and a new T-shirt in there for you," Libby called after him, her hands folding and unfolding nervously on top of the table. She took a deep, tremulous breath. What she'd seen in his eyes just before he'd disappeared into the bathroom had made her feel breathless, so totally alive. It had been a long time since she'd felt her stomach quiver, her nerve endings tingle from the look in a man's eyes.

She stared at the bed, wishing it didn't look so small, so intimate. This whole situation would have been so much easier had the room boasted a sofa, or a love seat...someplace where a person could stretch out and sleep instead of the bed. There wasn't even a bathtub, only a stand-up shower stall.

She paced around the room, looking into the drawers of the dresser, checking the contents of the kitchen cabinets, wondering how long they would have to remain in the small confines of the room before they could get back on the road. The room was small, and she had a feeling that with Tony's presence, it would shrink considerably.

She looked up as Tony came out of the bathroom. His dark hair stuck up wetly and he was clad in the new T-shirt and his jeans. "Whew, that felt good," he exclaimed, his eyes darkly inscrutable. Whatever she had seen in them moments before was now gone, smothered beneath a distant blankness that was somehow comforting to her.

"So...uh...what did you find out from your phone calls?" she asked.

Tony paced the room, quickly repeating what he had learned from Cliff, leaving out his friend's words of warning on just how dangerous the men were. There was no reason for her to know everything.

"So, what does this information tell you?" she asked when he was finished.

He shrugged and sat down on the edge of the bed. "It tells me it's more important than ever that we get to that lab and find out some answers about the necklace. If the men who want it belong to some sort of subversive group trying to take over the world, then we need to discover how this necklace holds the key.''

Libby nodded. ''At least we now have a name of somebody to talk to. Jonathon Maxwell...let's hope he has some answers for us.''

''Oh, by the way, I also talked to my neighbors. They're going to take care of your demon cat until we get back, and I called your ex-husband.'' Tony smiled. ''I've been fired.''

Libby laughed. ''He might have fired you, but I haven't. I have a feeling before this is all over I'm going to need my guardian angel more than ever.''

''I have a feeling we both need an angel in our pocket to get through this mess.''

''What's our next move?'' she asked.

''Sleep. Who knows what tomorrow will bring, so we'd better rest while we can.'' He walked over to the light switch on the wall, his eyes still dark orbs of blankness. ''I'll take this side, closest to the door,'' he said, pointing to the bed.

She nodded, reluctantly leaving her chair and approaching the side of the bed. She slid in beneath the sheets and looked at him expectantly. As he turned out the light and the room plunged into darkness, she moved over so she was lying on the outer inches of the bed. She didn't want a shoulder to bump, a thigh to accidently rub. She wanted to make certain she stayed on her own side.

She heard the whisper of a zipper and knew he was taking off his jeans. Her mind filled with an image of him without them, and she shook her head to dispel the erotic vision.

As the mattress sagged beneath his weight, she

squeezed her eyes tightly closed, wondering why her breathing was suddenly so irregular.

She could smell him—the clean scent of soap, the fragrance of the shampoo, and beneath that, the subtle scent of maleness that teased and taunted her.

Although he didn't touch her at all, she could feel the heat that seemed to radiate from his body, a heat she'd like to crawl into, remain in for eternity.

"Good night, Libby," he said, his voice sounding strangely full.

"Good night, Tony," she answered, wondering how on earth she would ever manage to sleep when all she wanted was for him to reach out to her and take her in his arms, drive her insane with his kisses and caresses.

Chapter 9

Libby awoke slowly, pulling herself away from the land of dreams and into reality. She cracked open one eyelid, noticing that the room was no longer pitch-black but held the deep gray of predawn. She knew Tony was still in the bed next to her, could still feel his warmth, could hear the throb of his deep, even breathing vibrating the bed.

She turned over cautiously to look at him. He slept on his back, his deep breathing attesting to the fact that he was sound asleep. She could see that she'd stolen the blankets from him at some time during the night as his legs were bare, sprawled apart in complete relaxation.

She knew she should get up or go back to sleep. She shouldn't be lying here staring at him while he slept. But she couldn't stop herself.

She'd known his legs were long, but she hadn't expected them to be covered with such fine, dark hair. And she hadn't anticipated the muscles that marked them with masculine shapeliness. The briefs he wore hugged him tightly, causing an intense heat to sweep through her as she moved her gaze upward. The T-shirt had ridden up his stomach, exposing the flat, tanned surface broken only by a narrow line of dark hair that disappeared into the top of his shorts.

If she reached out and touched him, would he awaken? By a mere touch on his stomach or thigh, would she stimulate a response she wasn't prepared to handle? She knew instinctively that his skin would be warm and welcoming. She also knew with a certainty that if she touched him in invitation, he wouldn't hesitate to take her. With men like Tony, love wasn't necessary…and it certainly had not been love she'd seen radiating from his eyes when she'd stepped out of the bathroom the night before. It had been lust…uncomplicated, blatant desire.

She rolled back over on her side, away from him. She wouldn't touch him. She wanted him, but she wasn't sure she was prepared to settle for what little he had to give. She squeezed her eyes tightly closed, hoping sleep would come again and bring peaceful oblivion, steal away the heated, erotic thoughts that danced provocatively in her head.…

Tony knew the exact moment when she fell back asleep. He felt her muscles ease into the mattress and her breathing resume a steady rhythm. He slowly allowed his own muscles to relax their tenseness. He'd awakened and instantly felt her gaze on him. It had taken all his control to maintain his aura of deep sleep. But he knew if he opened his eyes and saw her, he wouldn't be able to stop himself from reaching out for her.

And God knew, he didn't want to do that. If he was smart, he would not only get the hell out of this bed, but he'd get away from this woman, who was quickly gaining an obsessive status in his head. If he was smart, he'd run as far away from her as possible and never see her again. After all, this mystery was hers. She had the necklace. It was her problem.

He frowned, knowing that simply wasn't true. Yes, she had the necklace, but there was no way he could walk away from her and let her deal alone with the powers of the New Republic of Man.

However, he knew if he made love to her, continued to get more deeply involved, they both would lose. He'd seen firsthand the destructive powers of love. He didn't want to see Libby grow from a vibrant, strong woman to a shadow woman. He'd seen it happen to his mother, and he refused to allow it to happen to Libby. She deserved better than he had to give.

Another day or two and this mystery would be solved, and they would both return to their own lives. He could be strong for that length of time. He could fight his overwhelming desire to taste once again the sweetness of her lips, caress the shapely curves of her breasts.

She'd go back to her own life and she would eventually find someone who could give her all that she deserved, a man who wouldn't shy away from her love. And he would continue on his solitary path. He closed his eyes, wondering why this thought filled him with such an overwhelming ache of sadness.

The next time Libby opened her eyes, the morning sunshine streamed through the partially opened curtains and she was alone in bed. She sat up, pushing her hair off her face and looked around curiously. It was obvious she was not only alone in the bed but also in the room.

She got out of bed, spying a note on the kitchen table.

She scanned it quickly, unsurprised to discover that Tony had gone to the grocery store to pick up something for breakfast.

While he was gone, she quickly dressed and made the bed. She had just finished, when he returned, carrying a sack of groceries. "Ah, good, you're up," he said cheerfully. "I trust you slept okay."

"Fine," she answered, noting that the easy charm was back in his eyes, effectively hiding any deeper emotions he might have.

"I got sausage and eggs here," he said, unpacking the groceries. "And coffee and milk. In fact, I got enough supplies for us to hole up here for today and tomorrow. Oh, and here's a little something for you." He tossed her a box of Twinkies.

"Thanks." It was ridiculous really, how the fact that he'd bought her a box of the treats touched her. Most women received flowers from their male friends, but as Libby looked at the box of Twinkies, she realized they were more precious than a dozen roses could ever be.

She sat down at the kitchen table, watching as he efficiently sliced off the sausage and placed it in an old iron skillet he found in one of the rickety kitchen cabinets. As the sausage sizzled, he filled an aluminum coffeepot and got it perking on one of the burners. Within minutes a savory mixture of scents permeated the air.

Libby got up and crossed to the curtains, starting to pull them back all the way to allow the morning sun better entry.

"I don't think that's a good idea," Tony said softly. "We don't know how thorough these men will be if they're still looking for us. We don't want to make it too easy on them."

"Oh, of course," Libby replied, pulling the curtains

closed again. For a brief moment, she'd forgotten the men, the danger that still existed from them.

She sat back down at the table. "Do you really think we need to stay here for two days?"

Tony moved the perking coffee off the burner. "I don't know, Libby. I'm functioning in the dark as much as you are. I just think if we give ourselves a little time, say about two days, then our odds are better at not encountering those men. Hopefully by that time those men will think we got lost, or went back to Kansas City or left the country."

Libby nodded, wondering what they were going to do to wile away the next forty-eight hours in this tiny room. They couldn't go outside and explore the area. There wasn't a television—not even a radio—in the room. Just Tony, with his incredibly tight jeans, his evocative smile, his powerful maleness. It was definitely going to be a hellish two days.

"Sure you don't want at least a piece of sausage?" he asked moments later as he joined her at the table.

She shook her head. "Just the coffee." She took a sip and grimaced. "And I think one cup of it will be quite enough."

"Bad, huh?" He shook his head ruefully. "I never could make it without the benefit of a machine. But I did remember to get some lunch meat for sandwiches and hot dogs for supper. At least we can't mess those up with the antiquated cooking equipment."

She nodded, smiling as she watched him eat. He ate with a natural gusto, as if each bite might be his last. He would probably make love with the same passion, the same intensity. A woman would be loved thoroughly, completely, by Tony Pandolinni.

Libby mentally shoved these thoughts out of her head, knowing they were ridiculous and nonproductive.

She got up from the table and went into the bathroom, taking a cool, wet cloth and running it lightly over her face. She picked up the necklace from the edge of the sink and carried it back to the table with her.

As Tony finished eating, she focused her attention on the locket in the center, opening it and staring at the empty space within. "There's got to be something we're missing," she muttered. "Whatever is so important, it's not the necklace itself, and it's not what's on the inside." She looked up at Tony curiously. "What could it be?"

His brow wrinkled in thought. "I wish I knew."

Libby nodded her agreement and shoved the necklace aside.

After Tony ate, she helped him with the dishes, finding it strangely intimate to stand next to him at the sink doing something as mundane as washing dishes. His broad shoulders bumped hers as they put the dishes in the cabinets, the contact creating an electric circuit throughout her entire body.

With the dishes put away, Libby wandered the room and Tony sat at the table, tapping his fingertips on the tabletop. "Didn't you tell me that your father taught you to bluff at poker?" he asked suddenly.

She looked at him curiously and nodded. "Lots of times Vinnie and I would play cards to pass the time when business was slow at the shop."

Tony got up and went to the sack of items he'd bought at the grocery store and pulled out a pack of brand-new playing cards. "I thought these might come in handy."

Libby smiled eagerly, anxious to do something, anything to take her mind off the necklace and its danger, and Tony and a very different kind of danger. She sat down across from him at the table, watching as he un-wrapped the cards and shuffled them with deft fingers. ''We'll see what kind of a bluff you can pull off,'' he said, a twinkle of challenge in his eyes and a lazy smile of indulgence curving his lips upward.

An hour later, the indulgence was gone as he wit-nessed Libby's skill. Her eyes glittered merrily as she won yet another hand. Tony was playing poorly, and he knew he was playing poorly, but he couldn't concentrate on the cards in his hand. He couldn't think of anything but her scent, which seemed to invade his brain. He couldn't focus on anything except the memory of her mouth against his, hot and wild, sweet and hungry. He'd never wanted a woman with the intensity that he wanted Libby, and he feared the only way he would be able to get her out of his system was to make love to her, wildly, passionately and completely. Then, and only then, would he be able to stop thinking about her, stop wanting her, stop obsessing on what it would be like to possess her totally.

They stopped playing cards long enough to make sandwiches for lunch, then resumed the card games, moving to gin rummy, slapjack and even go fish.

It was after dinner that Libby shoved the cards away. ''If we play one more game, I'm going to be sick,'' she exclaimed.

Tony sighed, heartily agreeing. Still, the evening hours stretched before them, empty and tense. He got up and paced the room, trying to ignore the fact that sud-denly everything she did seemed overtly sensual, a taunt-ing turn-on. And the fact that she was oblivious to her effect on him only heightened that effect.

''I guess I'll go shower,'' she finally said, feeling a strange tension in the air. He nodded curtly, making her wonder if she had somehow done something to make him angry.

When she was gone and the sound of the shower filled the tiny cabin, Tony got up from the table and paced the room like a caged animal. He'd never done well at wasting time. He needed action, stimulation, something to take his mind off Libby.

He threw himself back into a chair at the table, feeling a foul mood descending around him, a foul mood that could only be lifted by an intense bout of lovemaking. He stared at the closed bathroom door, imagining her standing beneath the shower spray. He closed his eyes, seeing her body, lithe and wet, nipples distended from the stimulation of the shower spray. He saw himself, also naked, sweeping aside the flimsy shower curtain, joining her in the tiny enclosure. He'd soap her body, running the bar slowly, sensually down her neck, across each of her perfectly rounded breasts, down the flatness of her stomach and into the tangled curls of her center. He could hear her moans of pleasure, feel her wet heat surrounding him, taste the essence of her as his tongue followed his hand.

He shook his head, appalled to find himself standing at the door of the bathroom, his hand on the doorknob, his body fully aroused. Damn her...damn her for making him want her in a way he'd never wanted another woman. Damn her for complicating his life. He slammed his fist against the door in a rapid knock.

She threw open the door, her eyes startled, a towel barely covering the body he'd just been fantasizing about. "What? What is it?" she asked urgently.

"I'm going out," he said, backing away from the swirling steam that drifted out of the bathroom, backing away from the sweet, clean scent of her. "I'll be back later. Don't open the door for anyone but me."

Without waiting for an answer, he flew from the cabin, once outside breathing deeply of the crisp evening air, trying to regain control over his traitorous thoughts.

Libby finished her shower, then left the bathroom, shivering slightly as she remembered the blackness of Tony's eyes when she had opened the bathroom door and found him standing there. For a moment, for just a brief moment, she had thought he was going to grab her in his arms, throw her on the bed and have his way with her. She smiled at this thought, knowing that in having his way with her he would please her, as well.

She went over to the window and peered out. Darkness was beginning to fall and she wished Tony would come back. She didn't like the idea of being in this room all alone.

She got into bed, not knowing what else to do. She opened up the drawer in the dresser next to the bed and pulled out the only book the room boasted. This particular copy of the Bible looked like it had been read by hundreds and hundreds of people. The pages were yellowed, some torn, and she found herself wondering about the people who had rented this room before them. Had they been hiding? Or had some been lovers, come to find a night of pleasure in an off-the-tracks motel? She bet if these walls could talk, they would have hundreds of stories, slices of lives from people diverse and similar.

Where the hell was Tony? Where could he have gone? She jumped as she heard something outside the window. A thud, as if somebody had slipped and hit against it. She froze, tensed as she waited to hear if the sound would be repeated. Seconds ticked by...minutes...and still Libby didn't relax. She suddenly had a feeling that there was somebody, something just outside the window.

She slid off the bed and sidled across the room, holding her breath as she clicked off the light, plunging the room into darkness. All she could see was the faint outline of the window in the blackness that surrounded her.

Still holding her breath, she moved to the window and lifted the corner of the curtain a fraction of an inch. She stifled a gasp as she saw the shadow of somebody standing near the corner of the building. She closed her eyes for a moment. Let it be Tony, she prayed, afraid to look again, but afraid not to. She opened her eyes and looked once again, fear welling up in her throat as she realized the shadow couldn't be Tony, not unless he had grown an enormous potbelly since leaving the cabin.

She allowed the curtain to fall back closed, fighting off an overwhelming sense of hysteria. Who was out there, and where in the hell was Tony? In the darkness of the room, she carefully made her way over to the cabinets, opening a drawer and rummaging around until she felt the handle of a paring knife. She knew it wasn't exactly a lethal weapon, but at least with it in her hand she didn't feel completely helpless. She squeezed the knife handle, realizing her palms were sweaty. She moved back over to the door, waiting…praying for Tony to return.

Tony walked around the side of the cabin, immediately freezing as he saw somebody lurking in the shadows by the front door. He leaned down and eased his gun out, his adrenaline pumping through his veins, a welcome, familiar visitor.

He flattened himself against the rough wood of the cabin, narrowing his eyes as he watched the man, who seemed to be trying to look into the window. In an instant, Tony's mind took note of several different things. The man was vastly overweight and was breathing heavily through his mouth. He also didn't appear to have a gun or a weapon of any kind in his hands. Still, Tony knew better than to underestimate the man. If he was part of the group that was hunting them, he was dangerous and wouldn't hesitate to kill to get what he wanted.

Realizing he'd have a better chance of sneaking up on the man from the other side of the cabin, Tony eased himself around the corner of the building. With the stealth of a wild animal, he snuck around the back of the building, moving carefully so no twig, no branch would crackle beneath his feet and give away his presence. At that moment, he had the element of surprise on his side.

He didn't think anymore. He worked on instinct alone, allowing his years of police training to take over. He didn't think again until he was directly behind the man, his gun stuck in his back. "Don't move," he breathed softly as the man froze. "Don't move because I'm very nervous and you might make me shoot you."

"For God's sake, don't shoot," the man cried.

"Tony?" Libby's frantic voice drifted out of the cabin door. "Tony, is that you?"

"It's me, Libby. Open the door," Tony instructed, wanting to get the intruder inside, where he didn't have to watch his back.

Libby opened the door and turned on the interior light, its illumination spilling out to where Tony and the intruder stood. "Please don't move too quickly," Tony advised the fat stranger as he prodded him to go into the cabin.

Tony smiled at Libby, a dangerous glint in his eyes as he motioned for her to sit on the bed out of the way. "This gentleman seems to have an inordinate amount of interest in this room," he said pleasantly as he motioned for the man to have a seat at the kitchen table. His pleasant tone did nothing to diminish the fact that he was in control, and there was a cold calculation in his eyes that Libby had never seen before.

As he faced the man, Tony's gun didn't waver, but pointed directly at the fat man's belly. "Perhaps you'd like to tell us exactly why you are lurking around our room."

"For God's sake, man, put the gun away. I didn't mean no harm," the fat man replied, sweat running profusely down the sides of his ruddy face. "I was just supposed to find out if she was with you," he said, jabbing a finger toward Libby.

"Why?" Tony asked, all pretense of pleasantry gone as he eyed the man coldly. "What do you want with her and who sent you here?"

"I don't want nothing with her. I was just supposed to find out if she was with you. He told me he was sure you two were…you know…screwing around."

"Bill," Libby said flatly.

The fat man nodded vigorously. "I'm a private investigator. Bill Weatherby hired me to find you two."

"How'd you find us?" Tony asked, the dangerous lights in his eyes diminished somewhat. He still held the gun out, somehow enjoying the man's discomfort.

"I got a friend at the police department who overheard that you were here in Muddy Creek." He shrugged his massive shoulders. "There's only one motel around here, so you weren't that hard to find."

"You have ID?"

He nodded and reached into his breast pocket and pulled out a wallet. He flipped it open and held it out to Tony. Tony looked at the identification card, then thumbed through the rest of the documents in the wallet, satisfied that the man was indeed, who he said he was. He'd heard of the man before. Being in the same business, he knew most of the reputable and disreputable private dicks in the area. And what he knew about this particular man didn't make him a model of the profession.

"What's Bill paying for your report?" he asked.

"Five hundred a day plus expenses."

Tony smiled. "I'll make you a little deal." The fat man sat forward eagerly. "You go back and tell Bill you couldn't find us and I'll let you live." Tony's voice was deceptively soft, but his eyes held the hard glint of a man who didn't make empty promises. "You get the hell out of here and don't tell a soul that this is where we are, and I'll never bother you again. But if you tell one person that we are here, I'll find you wherever you are, and I'll make sure you never speak another word."

The fat man's face visibly paled. He cleared his throat several times. "Oh…as a professional courtesy, I won't mention to anyone that you're here," he agreed.

Tony smiled tightly. "As a professional courtesy, I strongly recommend you get into your car and drive as fast as you can back to Kansas City. You're lucky I didn't put a bullet in your back when I saw you at the window." Tony dropped his gun and motioned for the door.

The man moved with a speed that belied his bulky size, running out the door and disappearing into the darkness of the night.

"Should we leave here?" Libby asked as Tony shut the door and carefully locked it.

"I don't think so. I still think we're safe for the time being. It was luck and connections that allowed him to find us." He eyed the paring knife she still held in her hand. "What were you going to do with that pigsticker? Tickle him?"

She smiled ruefully. "It's the biggest knife in the drawer, but you're right, it wouldn't have done much against his protective layering." Her smile faded. "Do you really think he'll not tell anyone we're here."

Tony nodded. "He's a sleaze. He loves money, but he values his life even more. He won't tell."

Libby put the knife back in the drawer, then sighed in disgust. "I can't believe Bill hired that man. When will he quit?"

Tony eased himself down into a kitchen chair. Now that the adrenaline had fled his body, weariness took its place. "You picked a real winner to marry," he observed.

Libby turned and looked at him. "Yes, it's been my misfortune to be attracted to men who seem incapable of giving back real love." She stared at him for a long moment, wondering if she hadn't repeated the mistake.

Chapter 10

Tony awoke in the middle of the night. Somewhere, in a dark corner of the room, a cricket chirped in resounding monotony, but that wasn't what had awakened him. It was her heat, surrounding him as in her sleep her body sought the contours of his. She was wrapped around his back like a blanket, her scent surrounding him like a dream. For a long moment he didn't move, relishing the feel of her breasts pressed against his back, her legs spooned with his. He marveled at how well their bodies fit together, like utensils nestled together in a drawer.

Suddenly the intimacy was too much. He eased himself away from her and out of bed, seeking a chair at the table. Fumbling around in the darkness, he found his pack of cigarettes and an ashtray. Strange—since being with Libby, he'd nearly broken the nicotine habit.

He shook a cigarette from the pack, then changed his mind and threw the pack into the nearby trash can. Leaning his head back, he concentrated on all the reasons why he shouldn't wake Libby and make love to her. He genuinely liked her, and that was one of the strongest reasons for not making love to her. He liked her and he didn't want to hurt her.

It had never mattered much with other women. He could be a bastard, love them and leave them without a backward glance. He never stuck around long enough for anyone to develop a true case of heartbreak complete with scars.

Scars... He had enough from childhood to last him a lifetime. First, the scars of having a bastard for a father, then the scars from watching his mother lose her vitality, become colorless and without animation, eventually a shadow woman who had no life but what she could find in a bottle of gin. And the worst fear of all was that he truly was his father's son, with all his father's faults. He didn't mind being a bastard to women who didn't count, but he had promised himself a long time ago that he would never be responsible for making a woman a shadow, for sucking the life out of her and leaving her empty and bereft.

He thought of the private investigator who'd been sent on his way. The man had been an out-of-shape, greedy pig who'd do anything for a dollar. What bothered Tony was the thought that by taking the job from Bill Weatherby, he had put himself in the same category as the fat P.I. Lately, it was more and more difficult to remember exactly why he had wanted to quit the police force and go into business for himself. It bothered him that he could end up like the fat sleaze...taking whatever kind of job was offered for a few dollars' pay.

"Tony?"

He tensed at the sound of Libby's voice in the darkness. "I'm here," he answered after a moment of hesitation.

He heard rather than saw her sit up in bed. "Is everything all right?" Her concern was evident in her tone.

"Everything is fine," he assured her. "Go back to sleep."

She didn't go back to sleep. He heard the rustle of covers, the sound of her bare feet as they hit the floor. Then she stood next to him, her evocative scent all around him, the heat from her body surrounding him. "Are you all right?" she asked gently.

For just a moment he hated her. He hated her concern, he hated her beauty, hated her because he cared about her. "I'm fine," he answered tersely, wishing she'd go away, leave him alone.

"Can't sleep?" She moved even closer and he was afraid that if she touched him in any way, his tight control would break.

"Damn it, Libby, just go back to bed," he retorted sharply. He heard her sharp intake of surprise at his frigid tone, then the soft padding of her feet as she did as he asked. He breathed a sigh of relief. Good. Better that she think him a moody, cranky son of a bitch. Better that she realize he was a bastard. Better that, than let her see he was falling in love with her.

It was a long night, an even longer morning. Tony seemed to go out of his way to be surly. He snapped and snarled like a tethered dog who'd been teased by bullies, and it wasn't long before Libby found a foul mood of her own.

Like it's my fault we're stuck in this little cabin, she thought as she washed their lunch dishes. *Like it's all my fault the stupid necklace was brought into my shop.*

She looked over to where he sat at the table, staring blankly at the wall opposite him. She stifled the impulse to throw something at him.

She finished the dishes, then joined him at the table, drumming her fingertips on the tabletop, knowing she irritated him and perversely finding satisfaction in doing so. "I preferred your empty, charming ways to this surly, black mood of yours," she finally said, staring at him defiantly as he looked at her in surprise.

Slowly, almost imperceptibly, a twinkle appeared in his eyes. Damn, but she had nerve. Most people, when faced with one of his black moods, steered clear. But she met him head-on, unafraid of repercussions. "I'm sorry, I have been rather hateful," he admitted.

"Rather hateful?" She raised a pale blond eyebrow. "Try again."

"Okay, I've been totally hateful." He ran a hand through his hair. "I can't stand being cooped up in here. I'm used to action."

"This isn't exactly my idea of a fun vacation, either," she chided him.

He laughed, finding it impossible to hold on to anger where she was concerned. She simply wouldn't allow him to be angry with her for something that wasn't her fault. "I'm bored," he admitted.

"Want to play some more poker?" she asked.

He groaned. "I'm not *that* bored. Besides, you hurt my male ego yesterday by soundly tromping me."

"I know something we can do," she ventured.

"What?" he asked, knowing she didn't have on her mind what he did.

"We could play truth or dare."

Tony frowned. "What's that?"

"It's a game we used to play at slumber parties and

get-togethers when I was in high school. One person chooses to either tell the truth to a question asked, or do something on a dare.''

"Sounds stupid," he retorted, feeling himself growing more irritable with every passing moment.

"What's the matter, Pandolinni? Scared of a silly schoolgirl game?" Her eyes sparkled brightly.

"Fine, I'll play," he replied, smiling jauntily in answer to her challenge. "So, how do we start?"

"I'll start. Truth or dare?"

"Truth," he answered, wondering what exactly he was getting himself into.

Her blue eyes gazed at him directly. "Who was the first girl you ever kissed?"

"That's easy," Tony said with a laugh. "Her name was Linda Cooper and she was an older woman. She was in sixth grade, and I was in fourth, and I thought she was the most beautiful girl I'd ever seen. I was invited to a birthday party where she was also a guest and somehow we started playing spin the bottle." His eyes were a warm gray as he tilted his head to one side, a grin lifting his lips. "It was my turn, and I prayed and prayed for that bottle to spin to Linda and when it did, I thought I would die from happiness. I leaned over and kissed her, and she wiped her mouth and said 'Yuck!'" He laughed at the memory. "Needless to say, my infatuation with Linda died a harsh and brutal death." He eyed her with a wicked smile. "Now, your turn. Truth or dare."

"Truth."

"Who was the first man you made love with?"

Her face colored to a blossom pink. "Bill. Oh, I know it's dreadfully old-fashioned, but I was a virgin on my wedding night. Vinnie drummed it into me. 'Why would a man buy a cow if he's getting the milk for free?' he used to tell me over and over again, and to me it made a crazy kind of sense. Of course, I'm not so provincial now.'' Another blush swept over her face.

"Hmm, so you've had lots of lovers since Bill?"

"Not fair. One question at a time," she said with a teasing smile. "My turn again. Truth or dare?"

"Truth."

"Why have you never married?"

Tony folded his hands on the tabletop, gazing at them thoughtfully. "I decided a long time ago that marriage wasn't for me. The Pandolinni men really don't make good husband material." He looked back up at her. "Truth or dare?"

"Truth."

"Why did you and your ex-husband divorce?"

She smiled. "Bill wanted a very different woman than what I was. He wanted somebody who would be happy sitting at home waiting for his return. He wanted somebody to sit on the bench at his baseball games and ooh and ahh about his skill. I'm not a bench-sitter, never will be. To me, marriage is a partnership...a give and take. Bill didn't want to give. He only wanted to take." She pushed a strand of her shining blond hair behind her shoulder. "Bill will eventually be all right. He'll find the kind of woman he needs in his life and he'll move on. It's just a matter of time."

"Will you marry again?"

"Not fair," she reminded him. "That's two questions. It's my turn. Truth or dare?"

"Truth."

"Why do Pandolinni men make poor husband material?"

Tony frowned. He wasn't accustomed to talking about

himself, baring himself to anyone. *It's just a game,* he reminded himself. "My father was a great cop, but he was horrible as a husband and a family man. He was cold, detached. The characteristics that made him a good cop made him a miserable human being." His hands clenched into fists as he thought about the man he'd worked so desperately to please. "I joined the police force in an effort to make him happy, get some sort of validation from him. I watched my mother slowly fold into herself, escaping his coldness by warming herself with a bottle of gin." For a moment he forgot where he was, who he was speaking to, as memory after memory assaulted his brain.

"When I was in fourth grade, I noticed my mom getting quieter and quieter, and when she tucked me in at night, I'd smell the liquor. By the time I was in sixth grade, I smelled the gin when I got home from school in the afternoons. And when I was in high school, she rarely got out of bed. I hated her, but I hated my father even more, because I knew he was the one who'd created her. He'd made her a shadow. I finally quit the police force so I wouldn't become a man like my father, and I vowed I'd never take a woman into my life and subject her to the life-style that destroyed my mother." He jumped up from the table, suddenly angry that he'd said too much. "This is a stupid game and I don't want to play it anymore." He walked to the front door, needing to escape from her and her provocative ways and probing questions. "I'm going to see if I can't find a newspaper at one of the stores. I'll be back later."

Libby watched him slam out of the door, surprised that such an innocent question had obviously touched a nerve.

She ached for the little boy he had been, trying to

please a cold, distant father. She hurt for the child who'd never had his father and had lost his mother, as well. But more than anything, she mourned the man who had made himself a vow long ago…a vow created by disillusionment and bitterness.

Didn't he realize that by keeping himself isolated from love, by refusing to consider the possibility of sharing his life, he would eventually become a cold, detached man just like his father?

She hadn't meant to pry into his personal life, although she had to admit she'd hoped by playing the silly little game that she would learn a little bit more about him.

She got up from the table and grabbed her purse, digging in the bottom until she found her nail file. She had to do something, anything, to pass the time.

As she filed her nails, she thought of her shop, wondering what her customers thought about it being closed for the past two days. In all the years her father had owned it, and in the past year of her ownership, the store had never been closed during the week.

It was difficult to consider that three days before, her life had been sane and normal. Now she was in a motel room in the middle of the Ozarks, hiding out from men who wouldn't hesitate to kill her to get what they wanted. She was cooped up with a man she hardly knew, yet trusted with her life, a man she knew she was dangerously close to falling in love with.

She finished her nails and put the file away, then went to the curtains at the window and peeked out. Tony… She had a feeling there was a child within the man, a child afraid to reach out for love. And she didn't know how to do anything but love him. *Oh, Libby, you're such a fool,* she thought, letting the curtain fall shut again. Of all the men in the world, she had to be falling for a private detective whose personal demons made the men chasing them look tame. Damn, but sometimes life was incredibly unfair.

They ate dinner in silence, then cleaned up the dishes and put them away. "I'm going outside to look around," Tony said when they were finished. She nodded, almost grateful for his absence. There was a tension between them that she couldn't seem to dismiss, one that nothing seemed to dispel.

After he was gone, she went into the bathroom. She might as well get ready for bed. Hopefully they would get up early the next morning and get back on the road to solving this whole mess.

After her shower, she pulled her sleep shirt on. Perhaps it would be best if she was already in bed and asleep before he came back. Maybe that would ease the awkwardness of another night spent together in the intimate confines of the bed.

She got beneath the sheets and waited for sleep to overtake her. She'd just about drifted off when she heard the click of the door unlocking. "Libby?" he called softly in the darkness.

She didn't answer. Instead she didn't move, feigning sleep. She relaxed as he went into the bathroom and started the water in the shower. Her body tensed in anticipation as moments later she heard the shower stop, and she waited breathlessly for him to join her. She'd felt the sexual tension between them all day long, and now she sensed an explosion in the air, an explosion that seemed as inevitable as morning following this night.

He came out of the bathroom and even in the darkness she could feel the sudden energy crackling. She held her breath as he eased into bed next to her. She didn't move, knowing an accidental touch would destroy the tenuous control she had left.

She was aware of his breathing, not the deep, regular patterns of a sleeping man, but rather the short, shallow breaths that spoke of suppressed emotions. *We should be sleeping, preparing for tomorrow and whatever danger it might bring,* she thought. But how could she close her eyes and sleep with him lying so close to her, his heat surrounding her, enveloping her?

"Libby?"

She didn't know whether to answer him or not, but she had a feeling he knew she wasn't sleeping. "Yes?" she answered, surprised at the dryness of her mouth.

"Truth or dare?"

Again she hesitated, afraid to answer...afraid not to. "Truth," she whispered. She could feel his tension and her body reacted with a tension of its own.

"If I tried to make love to you right now...would you stop me?"

"No." The word seeped out of her on a breath of air that was caught in his mouth as he kissed her. His lips were hot, insistent, plundering hers with a hunger that overwhelmed her.

As his lips worked to devour hers, his hands slowly moved up the inside of her T-shirt, stopping to reverently caress the fullness of her breasts.

At the touch of his hands, Libby moaned into his mouth and arched herself against him, wanting to be closer, wanting to lose herself completely in the passion that exploded between them.

Tony wanted to take his time, to savor the sweet silkiness of her skin, the taste of her mouth. But as she sat up and pulled her T-shirt over her head, then beckoned for him to do the same, he knew there was no way he could control himself enough to take it slow and easy. He'd been beyond slow and easy before he'd even touched her.

He sat up and pulled his shirt over his head, gasping as her fingers immediately danced across his bare chest, raising hundreds of goose bumps of pleasure.

His mouth slowly nibbled down the length of her neck, licking and reveling in the small gasps and moans of pleasure she emitted. He wanted to pleasure her fully, he wanted to take her with him as he rode the tide to fulfillment. He wanted her to feel the same things he felt…and oh, was he feeling. His blood surged powerfully in his veins, and his heart thudded erratically. Every nerve ending in his body sang in anticipation.

She moaned again as his hungry mouth fastened on her breast, caressing and rolling the turgid nipple with the tip of his tongue. She tasted of honey and wine and forbidden fruit, and he feasted on her flavor, insatiable as an alcoholic drinking whiskey.

As he feasted on the sweet fullness of her breast, his fingers slid teasingly beneath the waistband of her panties. She felt her quickened breath, her heart flutter dangerously fast. Slowly he pulled the wisp of silk over her hips and down the length of her legs. Once she was completely bare to his touch, he took off his own jockey shorts, wanting her to feel the power and strength of his desire.

Then it was his turn to gasp and cry out in surprise as she took him in her hot hand, stroking him gently with butterfly caresses, forcing him to fight for control.

She moved beneath him, placing her hands on the broad expanse of his back, beckoning him to move over her, into her. With a throaty groan, he slid into her warmth, trembling violently at the exquisite sensation of velvety heat. For a moment he didn't move, simply remained buried in her glorious fire, afraid that he would shatter into a million pieces and it would all be over before it had truly begun.

Slowly he moved within her, closing his eyes as ripples of pulsating pleasure swept through him. She met his thrusts eagerly and her hands clawed at his back as if trying to pull him completely inside her.

His movements took on a frenzy as he buried himself deep and hard within her, and she met him with a frenzy of her own.

And suddenly she was there, and he was there with her. As she cried out, her body quivering, Tony shook with the explosion of his own release. He gasped and clung to her tightly, reluctant to let the feelings end. He'd never felt this way before, he'd never felt the sensations he felt at this very moment. And he was terrified that he would never experience them again.

Chapter 11

Tony awoke first, realizing instantly that the night had slipped away and the cabin was filled with the quiet of predawn.

For a long moment he didn't move, not wanting to interrupt the total tranquillity of waking well rested with Libby slumbering peacefully in his arms. He kept his eyes closed, enjoying the pleasurable sensations of Libby's curves molded against him, the scent of her hair tickling his nose.

He frowned thoughtfully. He knew that somehow a bridge had been crossed, a connection had been made between them. It was a connection that would make it impossible for him to escape from her unscathed.

When they finished with this mystery and went back to their own lives, he knew there would be many times when memories of this intimate time with her would come back to haunt him. There would be moments of reflection when he mourned what might have been if his ultimate decision had been different.

Still, he knew that to anticipate any sort of long-term relationship between them was a fool's dream.

They had come together, made their connection in the surreal world of a small cabin in the woods, surrounded by a heady combination of mystery, intrigue and danger. What they had shared here would never last back in the real world. He refused to make the same mistakes as his father and mother. As much as he hated to admit it, he feared he was too much his father's son to make and keep a marriage healthy.

He gently eased himself away from her and out of bed, studiously ignoring the desire to stand over her and watch her sleep. He stealthily crossed the room and disappeared into the bathroom, where he stepped into the shower. Maybe a hot, stinging shower would rid him of her scent, wash away the feel of her body against his, banish her from his thoughts and heart.

Minutes later he stepped out of the shower and dried off briskly with one of the thin, worn towels. He pulled on his jeans and T-shirt, his gaze falling on the thick gold necklace resting on the side of the sink. For a long moment he stared at it, frustration welling up inside. What did the damned thing contain? What in the hell was so important? With a sigh, he shoved it into his jeans pocket, then left the bathroom.

Libby still slept soundly, not having moved an inch since he had gone into the bathroom. Standing there for a moment, watching her in the dimness of the room, he suddenly felt the need to get on the road.

Her hair was like a halo surrounding her head and he remembered how it had felt in his hands the night before, with its perfumed silkiness and rich texture. She had given to him completely, holding nothing back as they'd made love. And he'd found himself responding in kind, unable to do anything else. It had been frightening...that moment when he'd lost himself to her, found himself in a veil of darkness where she was the only light, the only reality. He frowned.

She'd gotten too close, crept into his insides like a dreadful disease. The protective box he'd always kept firmly erected around his heart had been opened, and like Pandora's box, the mystery of it all scared the hell out of him.

He needed to regain his equilibrium, restore his self-imposed isolation. He needed to keep her out of his heart. He wanted out of this room, out of this mess that had brought them together. It was time to move on and bring this whole mess to an end.

He looked at her again. Despite his anxiety, he was reluctant to wake her out of her peaceful sleep. Besides, an hour more won't make any difference, he thought as his stomach rumbled its good morning.

He looked at his wristwatch. It was only a few minutes after five o'clock. If he woke her up now they would have time to stop at the restaurant for breakfast before they went on their way to Jasper Higgens's lab. Still he hesitated, knowing Libby would not appreciate being awakened at five o'clock just so he could have a hearty breakfast before they continued on their adventure.

His frown deepened as his stomach rumbled loudly. *Just because she doesn't like to eat breakfast doesn't mean I have to do without,* he thought irritably. He didn't want to wake her up or go to the trouble of cooking in the room, but as he remembered the wonderful steak he'd had two nights before at the restaurant down

the road, his mouth watered. They could probably fix
him up a dandy breakfast in no time at all. He could
probably eat and be back in the room before Libby even
awoke and knew he was gone. Finding a piece of paper,
he quickly scribbled a note telling her where he'd gone,
just in case she woke up before he returned. Laying the
note on his pillow, he crept out of the cabin and into the
brisk, fresh air of predawn.

Libby woke slowly, stretching sensually against the
crisp cotton sheets. She knew immediately that Tony
was no longer next to her. The heat of his body was
gone, but she could still smell the scent of his maleness
on the sheets, on her skin, and she closed her eyes and
smiled.

She couldn't remember the last time she had slept so
soundly. Her sleep had been that of a woman totally and
completely sated. She wanted him again, even now with
her body still tingling with the lingering sensations of
their lovemaking. She wanted him again and again. She
ran her hands down the sides of her body, remembering
the touch of his hands, the feel of his lips against her
skin. Making love with him had been everything she'd
imagined. He'd been a passionate, sensual, thoughtful
lover.

She sighed and rolled over, opening her eyes as her
hand encountered a piece of paper on his pillow. She
scanned the note quickly, smiling softly. Tony and his
morning appetite. She flushed slightly. His nighttime appetite wasn't too shabby, either.

She got out of bed and headed for the shower, knowing that the minute Tony returned to the room he would
be ready to hit the road.

As she stood beneath the spray of water, she wondered

what the day would bring. Would they discover the secret of the necklace? Would they find the answers they sought at Jasper Higgens's lab? And if they did solve the mystery and went back to their lives in Kansas City, what would happen between her and Tony?

Surely last night changed things, she thought hopefully. Surely after last night he couldn't deny that he felt something for her...that there was a magic between them. The thought of not seeing him again, not making love with him again, made a hollow ache of emptiness well up inside her.

But he'd been most emphatic from the very beginning. He wasn't looking for a long-term relationship. He didn't want a lifetime commitment. And what did she want from him? It was a question that, in her mind, had no clear-cut answer.

She shoved her head under the water spray, rinsing out the shampoo and unsettling thoughts. One mystery at a time, she cautioned herself. The first and foremost thing was to get rid of the necklace.

She had just finished pulling on her T-shirt and jeans and was towel-drying her hair when she heard the outside door of the cabin creak open.

"I'm almost ready," she called through the bathroom door. She quickly finger-combed her hair, looking one last time at her reflection in the mirror.

"I hope you had a good breakfast," she said as she threw the towel she'd used in the corner and walked out. "I figured you'd be anxious to get down to business and on the road and find—"

The last of the sentence strangled in her throat as she saw the albino sitting at the kitchen table, his pink eyes glittering and his thin lips pulled into a cold smile.

"Good morning, Mrs. Weatherby." His voice was

soft, but Libby heard the steely grit beneath the soothing tone.

"Good morning, Mr. Taylor," she returned, using the name Tony had learned from his friend Cliff.

The albino's eyes flickered in surprise at the sound of his own name. "Ah, it seems perhaps we have underestimated your knowledge. Unfortunately, we've underestimated several things, which has made us lose valuable time. But, I think all that can be rectified right now."

Libby's head spun and she swallowed hard, hoping to swallow back the frantic panic that made her knees weaken and her blood roar in her ears. She had to keep her wits about her. If only she could stall him until Tony came back. "What...what do you want?" she asked, glad that her voice betrayed none of the abject terror that twisted her stomach and produced a cold sweat to break out on her upper lip.

The man smiled. Again, it was a cold death mask kind of grimace. "I think you know what we want."

She reached up to her neck, startled when her hand encountered nothing. Where was the necklace? When had she last had it? Her mind raced, then she remembered. She had laid it down in the bathroom the night before when she had showered. It must still be in there on the sink. God, where was Tony? How long could it take him to choke down breakfast?

She gasped as Mr. Taylor pulled a knife from his pocket and with a barely perceptible click, a long, evil-looking blade popped out. "I grow impatient, Mrs. Weatherby. You and your friend have made us lose precious time. We're tired of the game. Where is the necklace?"

Libby licked her lip, surprised to taste the salt of perspiration. "If I give it to you, what's in it for me?" she asked, wanting to keep him talking until Tony returned. "I think a little negotiation is in order." She eyed him boldly, trying not to focus on the glitter of the wicked-looking knife.

"Sure, we can negotiate." The albino laughed, an unpleasant rumble that made chills dance up and down Libby's spine. "You give me the necklace without any problems or hassles, and I'll make sure your death is as painless as possible." His eyes narrowed. "However, if you make it difficult on me, I will see to it that your death is long in coming and your suffering enormous." He laughed again. It was the glee of a man who enjoyed instilling fear and causing infinite pain. "And before I kill you, I will possess your body in ways you never dreamed possible."

Cold-fingered fear grasped Libby's heart and squeezed with viselike strength. The thought of death was pleasant compared to the thought of his hands on her, touching her. A shiver of revulsion waved through her at the very thought. Dear God, what was she going to do? Her gaze darted around the room, looking for something, anything that could be used as a weapon.

"Don't go getting any ideas, little lady," he breathed softly, his eyes narrowing in warning once again as the knife in his hand twitched noticeably. "I can throw this knife in the blink of an eye and if I must, I'll pleasure myself with you after you're dead."

"Okay," Libby breathed slowly, her brain whirling desperately. "I'll...I'll get you the necklace...." She moved over to the small chest of drawers next to the bed. Pretending to open the drawer, in one swift, fluid movement, she picked up the Bible lying on the top and threw it with all her force at the albino.

She didn't wait to see whether she hit her mark or not. Instead, she stumbled into the bathroom and slammed and locked the door behind her. She panted, hysteria a whisper away.

The door was hit with a loud bang, and for the first time since she'd walked out of the bathroom and encountered the albino sitting at the table, she screamed. She screamed again as the door was hit another time with enough force to make it tremble in the wooden frame.

She could hear his muttered, vicious curses and knew that should he finally break into the bathroom, he wouldn't hesitate to use the knife on her. And she knew it wouldn't be a swift and painless death. He would torture her, and he would like it.

Another explosion against the door followed by a loud splintering sound let Libby know she had only seconds before the door gave way beneath the man's awesome rage.

I've got to get out of here, she thought frantically, eyeing the small window that was above the sink. The thick woods were right beyond the window. If she could manage to get out, she'd stand a better chance of getting away if she could hide in the woods.

She crawled up on the sink and strained to open the window, trying to ignore the loud, splintering noises that accompanied each bang on the bathroom door. She gasped in relief as the window finally slid open.

It was going to be a tight squeeze—the window was narrow and small. But she had to fit through. She *had* to. Without another conscious thought, she dove out the window, moaning impotently as she stopped halfway through, her hips wedged tightly in the frame of the window.

Panic clawed at her and she sobbed in desperation. She twisted and pulled, feeling the flesh of her hips skinning off in her frantic efforts. Tears streamed down her face as she heard the door behind her giving way.

Oh, God, how long did it take to die if you were stabbed repeatedly in the buttocks? she thought wildly. Her mind rebelled at the thought of this indignant death.

She renewed her efforts, death surrounding her. She would never get a chance to see Vinnie again. She would never have a chance to have children. She would never get the opportunity to tell Tony that she loved him.

With a desperate sob, she twisted her hips, stifling a squeal as she suddenly came loose and fell to the ground beneath the window. Without pausing, she ran for the cover of the woods, never stopping to wonder if Tony would be able to find her, never doubting that he would.

Tony kicked at a rock in the road and sighed with contentment as he walked slowly back toward the cabin. He'd had a delicious breakfast and was now anxious to get on the road. He looked at his watch, pleased to see that it was just a few minutes after six o'clock. With any luck they could be on the road within a half an hour and at the lab by seven.

As their cabin came into view, he tensed…spotting the dark sports car that was pulled up near the door. Libby! Her name echoed in his mind as he realized the danger that suddenly made his nose twitch nervously.

He pulled his gun from his boot and advanced slowly. His mind was suddenly blank, refusing to contemplate what had happened to Libby. He couldn't allow any emotions to thwart him. He needed to be clearheaded in order to help her…if she was still in a position to need his help. He gulped back a wave of nausea at this thought.

He dropped almost to the ground and advanced on the sports car, his gun ready to fire, his hand cool and steady from his years on the police force. The car was empty.

He eyed the cabin. The door stood ajar. He advanced cautiously, his ears finely tuned to any perceptible movement that would indicate somebody inside.

He moved the door completely open with his foot, keeping his gun ready in front of him. It took him only a second to see that nobody was in the room.

He relaxed his grip on the gun only slightly, sweat beading up on his forehead. He could still smell the evil of the man who'd been here. It lingered in the room like noxious fumes.

Where was Libby? His brow wrinkled in confusion as he thought of the empty car outside. If they had succeeded in taking her, why was the car still outside?

His heart leapt up into his throat as he saw the bathroom door, splintered and leaning against the door frame. It had obviously been beaten down, and his heart froze in his chest as he thought of Libby hiding in the bathroom, totally defenseless, completely vulnerable, praying for his return.

He pushed his self-recriminations aside. He had no time for that now. Instead, he eyed the tiny, opened bathroom window hopefully. Had she managed to escape through the window before they broke down the door? It seemed the only feasible explanation for the car still parked outside.

He looked at the window, hope flaring alive in his chest as he saw the tangled, wooded area directly behind the cabin. She was out there now, hiding, trying to evade the men that sought her. She needed him. He turned on his heels, his heart racing anxiously. She needed him, and God, he needed to find her.

Libby ran like the wind, afraid to stop, afraid to look behind her. Just as she had hit the ground outside the bathroom window and picked herself up, she heard the explosive sound of the bathroom door coming apart. She hadn't wanted to see if anyone was going to follow her, she had simply run, unmindful of the thistle bushes and thorns that tore at her.

Tears blinded her, along with panic, as she raced, stumbling over tree roots, ducking beneath hanging limbs. She ran as fast and as far as she could until the combination of thick underbrush and a painful stitch in her side made her slow down. Her chest heaved from her efforts and she took in large gulps of air. The sides of her hips were on fire where she knew she'd skinned and bruised them as she'd shimmied out the window.

At least I'm alive, she thought, but this did nothing to still the fear that remained deep inside her. Had she run far enough to lose the albino? Was he still following her, hunting her down like a wild animal? Should she continue to run until she dropped from exhaustion? Oh, God, she wished Tony was here to tell her what to do.

She stood completely still, straining to listen to the sounds of the woods. She was somewhat reassured by the silence that surrounded her. There was no crashing noise, no crunching of leaves beneath footsteps—nothing to indicate that somebody was on her trail.

She slid down at the base of a large tree, crouching down behind a fallen log in front of her. All she needed was a moment or two to get her bearings, catch her breath. When she had taken off running, she had zigzagged back and forth. Now she had absolutely no idea where she was. In fact, she had no idea in which direction the cabin was.

She wanted to cry. She needed to cry. But she had never been a noiseless crier, and the last thing she wanted to do was make a noise that would draw unwanted attention. Instead she chewed on her bottom lip, wishing she was back in the safety and warmth of Tony's arms. She wished she was back in her own little apartment with Twilight curled up at her feet. She wished she was anywhere but here. She wasn't cut out for this kind of stuff. She wasn't meant to be a hero.

From out of nowhere a huge hand reached from behind her and fastened firmly against her mouth. Libby's eyes widened in shock and her blood went cold. She stiffened, trying to pull herself away from the hand that held her tight. She gasped as a second hand snaked around her waist and jerked her upright against a taut, lean body.

"Shh, I'm here," Tony's voice whispered in her ear, and she sagged against him in relief, tears spurting from her eyes. She turned herself around and threw her arms around his neck, molding herself against him. She wanted to wrap herself around him, crawl inside of him, never let him go.

"Don't say a word, don't make a sound," he breathed into her ear, gently stroking her back reassuringly. "They're about a hundred yards from here." He pointed to the left. "We're going to circle back around and find the car. Then we'll get the hell out of here."

Libby nodded, still clinging to him in silent desperation.

"Uh...Libby. You're going to have to let go of me so we can walk," he whispered, tipping her face up with his finger. He kissed the tip of her nose, and she longed to crawl into the tenderness and caring that radiated from his dark eyes. "Are you all right?" he asked, tightening his grip on her for a moment.

Libby released a huge, tremulous sigh and nodded. As if by some unspoken communication, they moved silently through the woods together.

It took them almost an hour to get back to where their car was parked at the edge of the woods behind the cabin. It was the most excruciating hour Libby had ever endured. Twice they nearly walked into the men who hunted them. She shivered as they hid in the thicket, hearing the curses of the nearby albino.

When they reached Tony's Buick, the sports car was still parked in front of the cabin. Looking around cautiously, Tony and Libby jumped into their car and Tony started the engine with a roar.

He drove like a maniac, fast and frantic, needing to put as much distance as possible between them and the men who wanted them. Once again they kept off the main roads, instead going over trails and cow paths that kept them traveling in the general direction of the lab.

When they'd gone some distance with no indication that they were being followed, Libby's tightly controlled rein on her emotions gave way. Even though she wasn't aware of her need to cry, tears began racing down her cheeks, and her entire body trembled uncontrollably. She turned her head away from Tony, feeling ridiculously foolish as the tears continued to run unchecked down her face.

Tony reached out and pulled her over next to him, feeling the trembling that had seized her body. He put his arm around her, trying to absorb the trembling into his own body, imagining how frightened she must have been before he found her. She was so strong. She'd earned these tears. She deserved the release he knew they would bring.

"Everything is all right now," he crooned softly as she leaned against him weakly. He wanted to stop the car and take her into his arms. He wanted to hold her and stroke her until the horror was gone, replaced with sensations of passion and life. But he knew better than to risk pulling the car over. They needed to keep traveling while they had the slight advantage.

Hopefully it would take those men some time to discover that he and Libby had taken the car and fled. So instead of pulling over to comfort her, he did the best he could, hugging her close against him, stroking her hair and crooning words of assurance.

Within a few minutes, her trembling had stopped and her tears had dried, but she didn't move from Tony's awkward embrace. "Feeling better?" he asked softly, leaning over to press his lips to the top of her head.

She nodded, offering him a tremulous smile. "I guess I'm just not cut out for this kind of thing. I thought I'd die when I walked out of the bathroom and that…that man was sitting at the kitchen table."

Tony hugged her once again. "How did you get away?"

"I guess you could say I had the help of some divine intervention," she said, a small smile tugging at the corners of her mouth.

Again he marveled at her strength of character, her courage. "What do you mean?" he asked curiously.

"He demanded I give him the necklace and I pretended that's what I was going to do, then I threw the Bible at him." She looked at him, suddenly horrified. "Oh, Tony…the necklace…I don't know where it is."

"I have it," he explained, causing her to sigh in relief.

"So, tell me what happened after you threw the Bible at him."

"I ran into the bathroom and locked the door."

Tony laughed. "Honey, I've never seen anyone more cut out for this kind of thing than you. Quick thinking got you into the bathroom and away from those men."

"Yes, but for the past five minutes I've been a total basket case." She sat up and moved away from him.

Tony grinned at her. "At least you waited until after you were safe to fall apart. You handled it like a real pro."

"I don't want to be a pro," Libby protested tiredly. "I just want to go home."

Tony looked at her sharply, wondering if he had overestimated her inner strength. God knew, she'd been through hell the past couple of days. "We could turn around right now, go back to Kansas City. We could hand the necklace to the first cop we see and hope it gets to where it can do no harm." He kept his voice carefully neutral.

She hesitated a moment, her forehead wrinkling as she thought. "No, we can't do that," she finally answered firmly, a hint of renewed strength back in her voice. "We've come too far to turn back now. Besides, these people are really making me mad." She looked up at him, an impish gleam to her bright blue eyes. "I say we continue on, with one little condition…"

"What's that?"

"That for the rest of the adventure, no matter how long it takes, no matter how many days pass, you never eat breakfast again. Your breakfasts are definitely hazardous to my health."

Tony laughed and pulled her back firmly against his

side. ''That's a promise,'' he murmured into her hair, knowing that the most difficult thing he would ever have to do in his life would be to let this woman go…but that was exactly what he'd have to do.

Chapter 12

It was just after ten o'clock when Tony and Libby pulled up the narrow gravel road that led to Jasper Higgens's wooded retreat. The two-hour drive had been accomplished mostly in silence, but it had been a companionable one. They'd had to stop and ask for directions three times, and both were intensely aware that at any moment the powerful sports car could roar up behind them and shatter the tenuous peace.

Jasper Higgens's lab was nothing like what Libby had expected. She'd anticipated something white, large and clinical looking. Instead they found a two-story wood-shingled rustic house that nearly blended into the heavy woods surrounding it. What neither of them had expected to find was the house tightly boarded up and deserted.

At the sight of the heavy boards on the doors and windows, Tony closed his eyes and rubbed his forehead in frustration. "Apparently the agency handling this case has already been here and closed and locked everything up. Damn, we've come so far…endured so much, and for what?'' His dark eyes blazed with his frustration. He banged his fist on the steering wheel.

Libby reached over and touched his arm lightly, feeling an echoing despair as she looked at the house. ''I feel like Dorothy in *The Wizard Of Oz*,'' she said dispiritedly. ''We've followed the yellow brick road and fought off witches and goblins, and now the gates to Oz are locked and we'll never get back to Kansas.'' She looked at Tony expectantly. Strange, how in just a couple of days she had come to trust his judgment, depend on his initiative. ''So, what do we do now?''

Tony sighed and gazed once again at the house, then turned and looked at the surrounding grounds. ''Why don't we take a look around? Maybe we can find something or somebody who can help us. We need to figure out how to find Jonathon Maxwell,'' he explained. ''If this Maxwell fellow worked closely with Higgens, then he must live someplace nearby.''

Libby nodded and together they got out of the car and approached the silent, abandoned house. As she walked up the wooden steps that led to a large veranda, she felt strange and a little sad. Jasper Higgens's death suddenly seemed much more real as she realized this place was where the little old man had lived and worked.

Her heart constricted tightly as she saw a wicker rocking chair sitting by the boarded front door. The seat of the chair was broken in, as if it had been used many times.

She ran her hand lightly over the back of the chair, wondering how many times the scientist had sat in this very spot and viewed the beauty of the surrounding woodland. How many times had he sat here and contemplated his future, never knowing his fate was to be the victim of murder in an alley in Kansas City?

"He seems so real to me right now," she said softly, her hand lingering on the back of the wooden chair. "This is where he lived, where he worked and loved. Being here, it brings his death so close—" She broke off and looked at Tony.

Tony offered her a sympathetic smile and placed an arm around her shoulders. "I know how you feel. I used to feel the same way whenever I had to examine a victim's home, search through their personal belongings for clues to their murder." He paused a moment, remembering those days as a homicide detective on the force. "I always fought to gain an emotional detachment, to view the bodies as just bodies. Yet, touching their things, prying into their lives, I could never quite forget that they were real people, with people who loved them and people they loved." He shrugged his shoulders. "I could never quite get the emotional detachment I needed."

"Which probably made you a better cop than nine-tenths of the men on the force," Libby observed. She looked at him for a long moment. "You should go back to it, you know."

He looked at her in surprise. "Why would I want to do that?"

"Because you're too good to be wasting your time spying on ex-wives and chasing down lost dogs. You're one of the good guys, and you should be chasing down bad guys for a living." She leaned against the arm that encircled her and smiled up at him fully. She knew her love for him was there on her face for him to see, but she didn't try to mask or hide it. She wasn't sure she could even if she wanted to.

While she had been running through the woods earlier

that morning, fearing death at any moment, and later while driving in silent solitude, she had reached a decision concerning Tony. She loved him, and although she didn't know what tomorrow would bring, she meant to reach out and embrace every moment she shared with him. Life was much too short to worry about tomorrows and forevers.

When she and Tony got back to Kansas City and if they went their separate ways, it would hurt, but it would be a hurt that reminded her that she lived, that she loved. Until that happened, until he turned his back on her and walked away, she intended to hold nothing back. She would love him completely and with all her being. It was the only way she knew how to love.

"Come on, let's check around back," she said, grabbing hold of his arm. She saw the bewilderment in his dark eyes, a bewilderment tinged with fear and she knew he'd recognized the emotion on her face. "Come on," she said, smiling up at him. "Let's see if we can find any clues in the area."

Tony sighed with relief as she broke her gaze and tugged him around the side of the house. For a moment her eyes had spoken to him, telling him things he didn't want to hear, he couldn't accept. He didn't want her to love him. He didn't want the responsibility of her loving him.

She'd surprised him with her talk about how he belonged back on the force. Her words had echoed a sentiment he only allowed himself to think about late at night when he was discouraged about the slow growth of his private eye business. Perhaps when he got back to the city, it was a suggestion he should consider. He'd been less than happy since leaving the force.

As they followed the veranda to the side of the house,

Libby gasped with pleasure. "Oh, Tony, imagine having a view like this every day of your life," she breathed. He nodded, awed for a moment by the panoramic scenery before them.

Tangled woods and bushy trees formed most of a yard, and beyond that, a huge, glittering lake seemed to catch the sun's rays and reflect it back upward to the sky.

"It is beautiful," he agreed, his gaze spying a small clearing to the left that looked to be a helicopter landing pad. He frowned thoughtfully. Why had Higgens come to Kansas City? Why had he sold the necklace? It seemed a fairly good bet that he had known his life was in danger. What in the hell was the deal with the damned necklace? What could possibly be worth his very life?

He squinted, suddenly seeing a flash of movement from the corner of his eye. "Hey!" he yelled, vaulting over the railing of the veranda and dropping the four feet to the ground below, where he took off at a run.

"Tony?"

He was vaguely aware of her following his lead, catching up with him just as he caught up with a man in blue coveralls. The man held a lawn rake defensively before him.

"We don't mean you any harm," Tony said softly to the middle-aged, bald man, who didn't relinquish his hold on the rake. Rather, he tightened his grip, ready to use it as a weapon.

"You're trespassing," he said, his eyes sweeping over them both. Wary and suspicious, he slowly lowered the rake a fraction of an inch. "What do you want?"

"Do you work here?" Tony asked.

"I'm the gardener and handyman," he answered.

"The man who lives here is dead. Some policemen came and boarded up the house. I don't know nothing else."

"Do you know where we could find Jonathon Maxwell?" Tony asked, noticing the way the man's brown eyes flared slightly at the mention of the name. "He worked here as some sort of an assistant."

"Nope. I don't know any Jonathon Maxwell. I just take care of the grounds," he answered stiffly, his eyes not quite meeting Tony's steady gaze.

"Please, sir." Libby looked at him imploringly. "It's vital that we find Mr. Maxwell. It's a matter of life or death."

The man looked at her for a long moment, then shook his head slowly. "I'm sorry. I don't know anything. I just can't help you," he said, then turned to leave.

"Mr. Maxwell?" Tony called after him.

"Yes?" He turned and looked at Tony expectantly, then realizing what he'd done, he sighed and rubbed his balding head in frustration. "How did you know?" he asked Tony, his voice holding a weary resignation.

Tony pointed down at the man's feet. Beneath the old blue faded overalls, a pair of black leather dress shoes peeked out. "I've never known a gardener who worked in good shoes," Tony explained, then shrugged. "I just took a chance."

"Who are you and what do you want?" Jonathon Maxwell looked at them, tiredly leaning against the rake.

"I'm Tony Pandolinni and this is Libby Weatherby," Tony explained. "Somehow we've become involved in circumstances that relate to Jasper Higgens's murder, and now our lives are in danger." He pulled the golden necklace out of his pocket. "We want some answers."

Jonathon's eyes widened at the sight of the sparkling gold necklace. "Put that away," he ordered, his gaze darting around them nervously. "You don't know that we aren't being watched." He looked around, then gestured for them to follow him.

He led them down a small deer trail through the woods. Tony eased his gun out of his boot, not knowing where they were being taken, what they would find when they got there. His instincts told him to trust the man, but the stakes were too high to rely on instinct alone. As they walked, no one spoke. Tony felt his tension mounting, and when he gazed at Libby, he knew she felt the same, for her face was pale, her eyes large. Still she offered him a brave smile.

They left the woods near the lake's edge, and standing before them was a small fishing shack. It was into the shack that Jonathon led them. "Welcome to my humble abode," he said bitterly, gesturing for them to have a seat on the orange crates that served as chairs.

Once the three of them were seated, Jonathon began to speak. "I have a beautiful home and family less than six miles up the main road, but I haven't been home since Jasper's murder." His facial features tightened and he moved his orange crate closer to theirs. "There are men watching my house, waiting for me, and I have a feeling they don't want to wish me a happy day."

Tony withdrew the necklace from his pocket and dangled it in front of Jonathon Maxwell. "Those men are looking for this, and they have been extremely persistent."

Jonathon nodded slowly, his brown eyes looking like those of a deer, trapped in the sight of a hunter's gun. "Jasper told me once that he had given that necklace to his wife many years ago. He said if ever he wanted to hide something important, that's where he would hide it."

"But it's empty," Libby stated. "The locket is empty."

"Let me see." He took the necklace from Libby and turned it over. "Here on the back." He pointed to a small discoloration. "That's a microdot chip. It's what everyone is after." He gave it back to her. "Damn it!" He suddenly hit the side of the orange crate with his fist. He blushed, as if expletives rarely crossed his lips. "I'm sorry." He rubbed the top of his bald head with embarrassment. "It's just that Jasper was such a brilliant man, a genius when it came to chemistry and science, yet he was totally naive about people and power." His facial features fell into a small smile of sadness. "I guess that's what eventually got him killed. He trusted the wrong people and didn't realize his mistake until it was too late."

"What exactly do you mean?" Tony leaned forward eagerly. "Start at the beginning. What exactly is that microdot chip?"

"Jasper had been working on a particular project for years. It was something he deemed necessary for the continuation of the human race. When he was nearing completion of the project he put out a couple of feelers to find out who he should present the results to. He called a couple of old colleagues in Washington, D.C., told them what he was working on and the successes he'd achieved." Jonathon frowned. "I don't know who he eventually contacted or how it happened, but suddenly there were men hanging around the lab, and these were not upstanding citizens. They had guns, and mean faces and sly eyes." Jonathon looked at them, his own eyes tortured. "Jasper quit talking to me. It was like he knew he had made a mistake and he no longer knew who to trust."

"And this microchip…it holds the formula to whatever Jasper was working on… But why would he get rid of it at my pawnshop?" Libby pressed quizzically.

Jonathon shrugged. "I'm just guessing, but I suspect he knew he was in trouble. He wanted to get rid of the microchip and buy himself some time. He probably figured he could always come back and buy it back from you or at least remove the chip."

"So, what exactly was he working on? What's the formula for?" Libby returned impatiently.

"A formula that when injected into a person counteracts the effects of radiation sickness," Jonathon explained.

Libby looked at him in confusion as Tony gasped in shock. An antidote for radiation sickness? Why would anyone want to kill for that? How many people in the world could possibly be suffering from radiation sickness? She looked at Tony, surprised to see that his face was bloodless as he stared at Jonathon in horror. Apparently, he understood something that she had missed. "I…I don't understand," she finally said with frustration. "Who could want an antidote for radiation sickness?"

"Any group who wanted to take over the world." Tony breathed deeply. Seeing the confusion on her face, he continued. "Libby, think of the future possibilities of having such an antidote. If a group like the New Republic of Man possessed the antidote, they could plan to destroy all the world except those they wanted to live." His face blanched once again. "My God, they could set off atomic bombs all over the world, and while all the population was dying of radiation sickness, they would all remain healthy and in control."

As the realization sunk in, Libby trembled. A handful

of people would be in the position to pick and choose who would live and who would die, and the people doing that choosing would include men like the albino. It was a nightmarish thought.

"Why would Jasper Higgens even want to create such a formula?" she asked in amazement.

Jonathon sighed. "The uglier ramifications of such a formula never entered Jasper's mind. Several years ago his wife died from an accidental exposure to radiation. He was devastated by her death. He became obsessed with finding a cure for radiation sickness. I guess he thought he was doing the world an enormous benefit." Again Jonathon sighed. "It wasn't until the last day, before he left here, that he realized the people hanging around the lab weren't going to use the formula for the benefit of the world, but rather to rule the world." Jonathon reached out and touched Tony's arm, his brown eyes pleading in urgency. "Jasper had pretty well gone off the deep end when he completed work on the formula. I'm not sure it's viable, but you must make certain the chip gets to the proper authorities. In case Jasper truly was successful, you must ensure that it doesn't fall into the hands of these men."

Tony nodded to Jonathon in reassurance. "We held on to this necklace not knowing what it contained. Now that we know the importance of the formula, we will guard it with our very lives until we make sure it is given to the proper authorities." He looked at Libby for confirmation of his words.

She nodded soberly. She hadn't wanted to relinquish the necklace before just as a matter of principle, now she realized she couldn't relinquish the necklace even if her life depended on it. If Jasper Higgens had truly managed to develop such a formula, there was much more than her own life riding on the gold necklace. "How did they know where to find him? How did they know he'd placed the formula here on the back of the locket?"

Jonathon shook his head sadly. "Jasper made the mistake of keeping a diary. He'd written in it that he'd had the dot molded to the locket. It's my guess that when he left here to travel to Kansas City he was followed."

Libby turned and looked at Tony. "What do we do now?" she asked.

"I'll call Cliff and tell him what we know. He'll know who to contact, people who can be trusted. We'll set up a place and time where we can give them the necklace." He looked back at Jonathon. "Is there a working phone in the house?"

Jonathon shook his head. "The government men who were here yesterday cut all the wires and shut off all the power in the house when they boarded it up."

"Where's the nearest phone from here?" Tony asked tersely.

Jonathon frowned and rubbed the top of his head thoughtfully. "I guess the only place with a phone would be Walker's Grocery. It's a little grocery store and boat dock about a mile down the road. There's a pay phone in front of the store."

Tony looked at Libby. "We'll set up to meet Cliff at dawn at this Walker's Grocery. Let's get to that phone. I won't rest easy until we get this necklace to somebody who will know what to do with it." He touched Libby lightly on the shoulder and stood up. "Thank you, Mr. Maxwell, for telling us everything you did."

He nodded. "I pray you'll get it into the hands of good people." He paused a moment, then continued. "Jasper Higgens was a good man. He'd be devastated if he thought those other men would get his formula."

Tony nodded, pocketing the necklace once again.

Libby walked with Tony to the door of the fishing shanty, then turned back and looked at Jonathon Maxwell. He looked so helpless, so out of place with his intelligent brown eyes and bald head, sitting on an orange crate in the small shack. "Will you be all right?" she asked with concern.

Jonathon nodded, again with his small, shy smile. "I'll be fine. As soon as the necklace is with the proper authorities, the men watching my house will go away and I'll be able to go back home. In the meantime, I'll be safe here." He offered her a reassuring smile.

Libby returned his smile, then turned and joined Tony. Together they left the laboratory assistant and the small fishing shack behind.

Hawk could feel the albino's anger when they finally realized the woman and the private eye had escaped. Although the albino spoke not a word, his silent rage was a living palpable force in the car as the two men traveled toward Higgens's lab. It smelled like the spoor of a wild animal, savage and ugly.

"We'll catch up with them at the lab," Hawk stated emphatically. "If you'd stuck with me when we got to the motel, we would have had them." The damn fool had rushed things by going into the cabin alone. He always wanted it all for himself, he thought. He steadied himself and continued, "We have nearly fifty men in the area. They won't escape."

The albino turned colorless eyes to Hawk. "No matter what happens, no matter what comes down...the woman is mine." The emotionless tone of his voice didn't invite argument.

A momentary flare of compassion touched Hawk's

heart as he thought of the beautiful, blond-haired Libby Weatherby. Her death would not be pretty. She had made a deadly mistake when she'd incurred the wrath of the albino. She would pay a dear price for her error.

The flicker of compassion instantly died, finding infertile ground in Hawk's hardened heart. He was interested only in the necklace and the formula it contained. If people died in the process of obtaining that formula, well...such was the price of power.

Chapter 13

Tony pulled the car to a halt down the road a ways from Walter's Grocery and Dock. "I'm going to let you off here," he explained, pointing to the thick woods near the car. "I'll go hide the car where nobody will find it. If they can't see it they won't know for sure where to look for us." He reached out and touched her wrinkled brow gently. "Don't worry. I'll ditch the car, make the phone call to Cliff and be back here within an hour."

"I'll go with you," she protested, and he knew she didn't want to be left alone in the woods again.

"Libby, that isn't practical. Those men could find us at any moment. It's obvious they have a network of people working with them. I can move faster on my own and I'd feel better if I knew you were here, safe and sound. You wait here for me. Stay off the main road and stay out of sight," he instructed as he reached across her and opened her car door.

"Hurry back," she said softly, then turned to him and kissed him fully on the lips.

Tony held back only a moment, then he kissed her hungrily, returning the fervor, the intensity. He finally pulled away from her, looking into the blueness of her eyes. "I'll hurry back." He smiled softly. "Don't you remember? I'm one of the good guys."

She nodded, pressing her lips against his scruffy, whisker-darkened cheek.

Tony held her close for a moment longer, feeling the tightening of his muscles as passion fought against cold, common sense. He would have loved to linger here, take her into his arms and make love to her in the back seat of the car. But he had to go now...before the albino caught up with them. He needed to get in touch with Cliff immediately and get something set up. He couldn't afford to dally. Time was of the essence.

"Libby," he said gently, breaking their embrace. "I've got to go." He pulled the necklace out of his pocket and fastened it securely around her neck. "I don't want anything to happen to this. If I don't return, you go down to Walker's Grocery at dawn tomorrow morning. Somebody will meet you there."

"You'll be back," she said firmly, as if the idea of his not returning was totally intolerable. Without another word, she got out of the car and, blowing him a kiss, she disappeared into the thick brush at the side of the road.

What a woman, Tony thought as he put the car into gear and took off down the dusty, gravel road. No scenes, no tears; she had accepted the fact that he had to leave. She would have made a mighty fine policeman's wife. He sat up straighter in the seat and frowned. But he was no longer a policeman and the very last thing he needed to be thinking about was Libby's qualifications as a candidate for a wife. He didn't want a wife.

It was better to hurt a little now and stop the love that had flowered between them before it burst into full fruition, then rotted from neglect on the vine.

Tomorrow the necklace would be handed to the proper authorities, and they would go back to Kansas City. Libby would go back to working in her pawnshop, and he would immerse himself in his work.

"It's best this way," he muttered to himself, pulling up in front of Walker's Grocery. He shoved all thoughts of Libby to the back of his mind as he spied the pay phone on the side of the little store.

Libby looked around with satisfaction. She had found the perfect place for her and Tony to spend their time until morning came and they could unload the necklace. She had stumbled on the small hiding place quite by accident.

When Tony had let her out of the car, she had walked for several minutes, wading through tall weeds and fighting thick underbrush. Finally, knowing she was far enough off the road for safety, she'd sat down to wait his return.

Ahead of her was a grove of evergreen trees. The trees grew straight and tall, but the bottom of their trunks were obscured by tangled vines and thick brush. She'd been sitting, staring at them blankly for several moments when she realized there was a small break in the undergrowth that looked like a small, inviting door.

On impulse, she scrambled to her feet and made her way to the small, nature-made doorway. She got down on her hands and knees and crawled through. She sat back on her haunches and looked around, satisfaction welling up in her heart.

It was like being in a very small room, with the overhanging boughs above forming a ceiling and the thick bushes and tangled underbrush forming walls. The floor of the tiny area was covered with brown pine needles that had fallen throughout the winter months and now made a comfortable, soft carpet beneath her knees.

She lay down on her back on the carpet of soft needles, gazing upward, where glimpses of the brilliant blue sky could be seen through the overhanging pine boughs.

It was a beautiful day, but the beauty was somehow tainted by the knowledge that this would be her last day and night spent with Tony. Tomorrow, if all went as planned, they would return home to Kansas City. And what would happen then? What would happen to the tenuous connection she and Tony had made? Would they lose each other when they got back to reality...away from the surreal world they'd existed in for the past couple of days?

She closed her eyes, remembering the lovemaking they had shared the night before. They had fit together as if they were two halves of a whole, as if they belonged in each other's arms.

Even now, just thinking about the magic of his kisses, the mastery of his caresses, that moment when he'd entered her with all his heat and strength, she felt an answering response in her own body. She sighed, a soft whisper of longing. Could this love she felt for him override the fear his parents' marriage had built in him? Could she make him forget fear and learn to trust in love and the concept of forever? For she couldn't settle for less than that. For her, it was either all or nothing. She'd never given herself halfway to anything in her life, and she wasn't going to do it with Tony.

Her hand reached up and touched the necklace that lay cold and alien around her neck. She wanted to hate its very existence for all the greed and death it represented. Yet, how could she hate the very thing that had brought Tony to her?

Would it also be the thing that put an end to their love forever? A stab of cold, harsh fear coursed through her at the thought. What if the albino and that other man caught up with Tony before he had a chance to ditch the car and get back to safety? She knew Tony would die before he told them where she was, but this thought brought no comfort.

If she and Tony went back to Kansas City and she never saw him again, she could accept that, knowing he was alive. But if something happened to him and he didn't make it back to her now, she knew she would live with an empty ache deep inside her for the rest of her life.

"He'll be back," she said softly with calm reassurance. After all, the good guys always returned.

Tony hid the car in a ravine about two miles from where he had left Libby. He'd made his phone contact with Cliff and set up a rendezvous for dawn. He was confident Cliff would know who could be trusted. As he jogged down the gravel road, he looked down at his wristwatch. Almost one o'clock. Approximately sixteen hours before they would meet Cliff and his associates.

Tony's eyes narrowed as he saw a cloud of dust ahead, signaling to him the approach of a car. He dove into the brush at the side of the road and lay motionless.

The car was a brown Toyota, and it approached at a

snail's pace. Tony's heart thudded loudly as the car passed within twenty feet of where he hid. He was close enough to the side of the road to get a good look at the occupants. They didn't look like a typical couple out for a Sunday drive.

The two men in the car were big and burly, and the one on the passenger side had a gun pointed out the window. They were headed toward the grocery store where Tony had just been, and his nose told him they were looking for Libby and him. Obviously they were drones of the New Republic, and they didn't look like nice men.

Once the car was out of sight and the cloud of dust had disappeared, Tony hit the road again. He stepped up his pace, anxious to get to wherever Libby hid. Thank God he'd decided to dump the car. He was certain the entire network of the New Republic group had a description, and probably the license plate number of his car. He and Libby would have been sitting ducks had they remained with the vehicle. As long as those men were looking for the car, maybe he and Libby would be safe.

"All we need is sixteen hours," he said aloud, pacing the words to match his running footsteps. He didn't want to think about how many things could go wrong in the space of sixteen hours.

He slowed down as he came to the place in the road where he had let Libby out of the car. Even though the scenery by the side of the road all looked pretty much the same, Tony had marked the position in his mind by noting a brilliant patch of yellow wildflowers on the left and a lightning-struck tree trunk in the distance. He left the road at this point and made his way through the thick underbrush.

Almost immediately he began whispering Libby's

name, wondering how far she might have wandered through the woods before coming to a place to stop. He walked and called to her for several minutes, then stopped as he heard her answer.

"Libby?" he called softly, looking around curiously.

"I'm here, Tony," she answered, but he didn't see her anywhere. He tried to follow the direction of her voice, but the surrounding trees and brush distorted it, and he couldn't tell exactly where the sound of her voice came from.

"Libby, where are you?" he asked impatiently, straining his eyes to catch a glimpse of her.

She laughed, a wonderfully rich sound that made him smile in return. "I found a marvelous hidey-hole," she said.

"Wouldn't you like to share your marvelous hidey-hole?" he asked, his eyes narrowed as he scanned the area. He was surprised that he saw not one single sign of her...not a glimpse of her T-shirt, not a strand of pale, blond hair. Wherever she was hiding, it was definitely a good place.

He jumped in surprise as her head suddenly appeared in a small opening in the brush not ten feet from where he stood. "Come into my home, said the spider to the fly." She gave him a small smile, the look in her eyes speaking of the relief she felt at his appearance.

Tony wiggled through the small opening, then sat cross-legged on the soft carpet of pine needles and looked around in amazement. "This is perfect," he exclaimed.

"Did you have any problems getting rid of the car?" she asked.

Tony shook his head. "I found a small ravine about two miles away. I parked the car there, then pulled some fallen branches and limbs over it.'' He grinned ruefully. ''I'm not exactly experienced in the art of camouflage, but the car isn't visible from a distance.'' He frowned slightly. ''We'll have to keep very quiet because this New Republic group are on the lookout for us. Let's just hope they keep looking for the car and don't suspect that we've ditched it and are now on foot.''

Libby shivered, and Tony moved closer to her and placed his arm around her slender shoulders. ''Stay strong a little bit longer,'' he whispered softly. ''We'll meet Cliff first thing in the morning and hand over the necklace. Then we can get back to our normal lives.''

Libby nodded, cuddling closer into his arms. ''It will seem sort of strange being just an ordinary pawnshop owner after being in the middle of a national security threat.''

Tony looked down at her with a grin. ''Libby, you will never be just an ordinary pawnshop owner.'' He leaned down to kiss her but stopped as his stomach rumbled loudly, causing her to laugh. ''I've been trying to ignore the fact that I'm starving,'' Tony exclaimed. ''But unless I like pine needles, I guess we'll just have to wait until tomorrow morning when all of this is over.'' He groaned at the thought. ''God, sixteen hours without food.''

''The best thing for us to do is keep ourselves occupied and not think about food,'' Libby observed.

''How are we going to do that? We've got sixteen hours to occupy with no television, no radio, nothing to pass the time. I left the deck of cards back in the motel room.'' He ran a hand through his thick, dark hair. ''Waiting was never one of my virtues,'' he admitted.

''I can think of one way to pass the time,'' Libby said after a moment of hesitation.

He looked at her curiously. "What's that?"

Moving out of his arms for a moment, Libby smiled at him, a sexy smile that instantly made his blood race a little faster in his veins. With one fluid movement, she pulled the T-shirt over her head and looked at him expectantly.

Tony's physical reaction was swift and intense. "Oh, Libby Weatherby..." He sighed. "Sometimes you have the most marvelous ideas," he murmured as he drew her back into his arms.

He didn't think about what might happen in the next twenty-four hours, he didn't think about what would happen when they got back to Kansas City. He certainly didn't want to think about what a bastard he would be to make love to her once again, knowing there would never be, could never be, a future with her. All he thought about was Libby and his need to love her one last time.

His mouth was hard against hers, his tongue delving deep within. She kissed him back, reaching her hands up to tangle in his thick hair, wanting him with a fever that threatened to make her ill.

She helped him tug off his T-shirt and they both shrugged out of their jeans, coming back together naked and eager, but caressing slowly, exploring the mysteries they might have missed in the darkness the night before.

As he took his fingers and traced the rounded swell of one of her breasts, his eyes sought hers, and she saw the fires that lit their darkness. "You're beautiful," he whispered as his fingertips rubbed her swollen nipple.

"So are you," she answered, reaching down and taking him in her hand, loving the feel of velvet heat, softness and strength. She stroked him gently, feeling the answering pulsating sensation, reveling in the fact that she was responsible for his powerful passion.

She gasped in pleasure as his mouth covered her breast, wet and hot, causing ripples and tingles throughout her entire body.

The afternoon sunshine danced through the thick pine boughs overhead, raining golden shafts of light onto their bed of pine needles. Even as Libby was slowly, deliciously losing her mind beneath his masterful caresses, she noticed the way the sunlight danced in his dark hair, whispered along the taut tendons and muscles of his back. And as he moved away from her breasts, his tongue licking and teasing first her flat abdomen, then lower to her thighs and finally at her very core, the sunshine overhead disappeared, instead burning brightly within her. She writhed beneath him, his expert caresses sending her falling, tumbling into a vortex of sensation, convulsing with wave after wave of pleasure so intense she feared she would die from the glory.

"Please," she whispered, wanting him inside her, filling her with his love. With a groan, he moved over her, plunging into her. She gave a small cry and wrapped her legs around his narrow hips, pulling him deeper within her.

His rhythm was slow at first, letting her savor the gliding motion of his heat against hers. She looked up into his eyes, and she saw his love there in the glittering dark depths, the love he refused to acknowledge, the love he refused to welcome into his heart. He could deny his feeling for her all he wanted, but she saw it and it filled her up as completely as his body filled her physically.

Tony was lost...lost in her moist warmth, lost in the sweet taste of her, the scent of her. He wanted to move slowly, linger over each exquisite sensation, but his control was gone. Her hands moved frantically over his back, her legs wrapped tightly around him, urged him to pick up the pace. He plummeted into her wildly, frenzied with need, shaken with the tremors that possessed him.

He felt her tighten around him, felt her body convulsing as she gasped in surrender, and suddenly he was there with her, emptying into her warmth, shattering his reality, discovering that in filling her, he filled himself.

Afterward, they lay in each other's arms, their nakedness feeling completely natural in this secret room of sorts that nature had provided as a retreat in which they could hide.

She fell asleep first, cradled in his arms, her heartbeat conversing with his own. Her body molded to his, her soft breath warming his neck. Tony closed his eyes, trying desperately to erect the barriers that had always kept him safe before. She'd somehow gotten through the fortress he'd always kept around his heart. She'd managed to touch him in the place he'd always guarded so possessively. And the most frightening thing of all was that he didn't know what he was going to do about it. With a heavy sigh, he allowed sleep to overtake him.

He awoke at dusk, the reds and oranges of the setting sun dusting the woman in his arms in fiery hues. His skin was cooled by the evening air everywhere but where her body touched his, and in those places was a warmth that pierced through to his heart. Her beauty astonished him; her strength awed him. She was everything he would want, if he wasn't so sure it was best he remain alone.

As he stared at her, her eyes fluttered open and she smiled, the soft, gentle smile of a woman in love. "Hi," she whispered, reaching her hand up and laying her palm on the side of his face.

"Hi," he answered, and his heart seemed to stop beating for a moment as he gazed into the honest blue depths of her eyes.

"Tony..."

He placed a finger to her lips. He knew the words she was about to speak. They shone from her eyes, and he didn't want to hear them. "Don't say it. For God's sake, don't say it." He gently extricated himself from her and reached for his T-shirt. As he dressed, he was aware of her gaze on him, level and probing.

"By not speaking of it, it doesn't go away," she said, reaching for her own clothes. When they were both dressed, she touched his shoulder. "I love you, Tony."

He closed his eyes. He hadn't wanted to hear the words. He hadn't wanted to accept the responsibility for her feelings. "Libby...I've made it clear from the very beginning that I'm not in the market for a relationship." He sighed tremulously, not looking at her. "I should have maintained some control over the situation. I guess I led you on," he finished inadequately.

"You didn't lead me on," she protested softly. "You made no promises, you inferred nothing. I did only what I wanted to do. I guess I didn't want tomorrow to come without you knowing how I feel about you." She paused a moment then continued, "And I think if you look in your heart, you'll realize you love me, too."

Tony took a deep breath, knowing if he was going to put an end to this, it had to be now. "Libby, I love how we make love together, but I think you're mistaking lust for love." His words affected her like a slap across the face, and he fought the impulse to take her in his arms and erase the look of hurt that streaked across her features.

"I don't believe that," she answered, her gaze still level, forcing him to finally look away.

"Libby, I quit my job on the force so I wouldn't become like my father. I promised myself I'd never marry so I couldn't do to a woman what he did to my mother."

"But you aren't your father," she protested, once again touching his arm. "And I'm not your mother."

He looked at her searchingly. "But how long before you become her? How long before you fade into the shadows, let unhappiness eat you up inside?" He shook his head firmly. "No...I won't allow history to repeat itself. I've always been alone, and I'll remain alone."

"You're a fool, Tony Pandolinni," she answered, her blue eyes flashing as anger swiftly usurped the hurt. "You're a damn fool to turn your back on what we've found together." These were the last words she spoke. She curled up on her side, but he knew she didn't go back to sleep.

This is for the best, Tony thought. *When we get back to Kansas City, we'll go our separate ways. Eventually she'll find another man to love, to build a life with.*

She had an incredible capacity to love. And he would go back to his solitary life.

It was all settled, all decided. He was absolutely certain that he'd done the right thing, made the right decision. What he couldn't understand was why in making the right decision, he suspected he was closer to being his father's son than he'd ever been in his life.

Chapter 14

"Shh."

Libby came awake immediately, feeling Tony's hand pressed tightly against her mouth, his body lying directly on top of hers. She lay still, listening to the snapping, crunching sounds of somebody walking outside their little hiding place. The noise of heavy footsteps was close, too close for comfort. Somebody was walking just on the other side of all the vines and brush. The beam of a high-powered flashlight swept across the overgrowth behind which they hid.

She closed her eyes tightly, fear making her heart thud loudly in her ears. She wondered if Tony could hear the frantic beating of her heart. It sounded to her like it was beating loud enough to alert whoever was on the other side of the bushes.

Tony's body was hard and taut against hers, his muscles tightened with tension, as if anticipating the need to jump up and fight, or run. He stiffened as first one voice, then another called out. There were at least three men out there, and Libby had a feeling they weren't out looking for mushrooms.

Horrible visions played in Libby's mind, as if on a large movie screen. The only difference was that in a theater she'd be able to close her eyes and make the picture disappear—but now, eyes open or closed, the images remained. The visions were all the same...the albino, with his cold, deadly eyes, and his sharp knife glittering wickedly. She remembered the sound of his rage when she had managed to evade him and lock herself in the bathroom. His anger had been an awesome force, and Libby shivered uncontrollably at the thought of finding herself at the mercy of his rage.

As she shivered, Tony pressed down more firmly on top of her, as if to still her shivering with his own body. His weight only managed to force the air out of her lungs, making it difficult for her to breathe. Yet she was grateful for the weight of his body, for with his strength and warmth pressed against her, she almost felt safe.

She wrapped her arms around him tightly, wanting to hold on to him forever. She wanted to pull herself up inside of him and hide there until the danger had passed. She had never known that fear could taste so bad—she could taste it now, and it was something she hoped never to taste again.

Seconds passed, minutes...minutes that felt like years, but finally the footsteps moved away, and the voices receded deeper into the woods. Tony eased his weight off her by raising up on his elbows, then gazed down at her, and she was suddenly aware of his heart beating as rapidly as her own.

She was also aware of the fact that night had passed while she slept, and the world was illuminated with the first stirrings of dawn. She looked up into Tony's face, wanting to memorize each line, every feature. She wanted to remember him the way he looked at this very moment. His chin was darkened with the stubble of whiskers, and dried pine needles clung to his dark hair, but it was the look in his eyes that she wanted to remember for the rest of her life. For in his eyes, she saw the love she felt for him reflected back to her. His onyx eyes reflected his vulnerability, and his love for her. Her memory of his denials from the night before faded. He loved her. She knew he did.

Neither of them spoke a word as his lips slowly descended to hers. He kissed her deeply, passionately, with all the emotion he had not spoken of the night before.

When the kiss finally ended, she looked at him with sad longing, recognizing the kiss for what it had been— a goodbye.

"You're a damn fool," Libby whispered softly, and Tony nodded.

"It's time to go," he said, releasing his hold on her and sitting up. "We've got to get to Walker's Grocery, and we're going to have to be very careful. They're looking for us."

Libby nodded and followed him as he crawled through the doorway of the brush. "Stay right behind me and don't make any noise," he warned in a whisper, reminding her that they were not out of danger yet.

She did as he instructed, staying behind him as they moved through the woods in the direction of Walker's Grocery and Dock. She had no sense of direction and was grateful that Tony moved through the semidarkness with the assurance of a born trailblazer, pausing only once momentarily to get his bearings.

As Libby followed him, she thought of the past week

of her life. She had been robbed and assaulted, had faced danger and death, yet she knew these memories would eventually fade. It was the love she had discovered that she would find difficult to forget. Her bruised neck, her scraped hipbones—those injuries would eventually heal, but her heart would forever carry the scars of her adventure.

Tony stopped suddenly as they neared the edge of the woods. Ahead of them was the grocery store. It was closed. Not a light shone from within, and the small parking area in front was empty.

"Where are your friends?" Libby whispered, dismayed to find nobody waiting for them, no friendly faces waiting to take the necklace from them and relieve them of their deadly burden.

"It's still early," Tony whispered back, his eyes searching the eastern skies where the sun was reaching out with tentative fingers of light.

He scanned the area, searching out the best place for them to hide and await Cliff and his people. He didn't like being this close to the store, where anyone could sneak up on them from any direction. His gaze landed on the large gas pumps at the end of the long boat dock. If they could make their way down there, they could hide behind the pumps. They wouldn't have to watch their backs because their backs would be to the open lake.

He eyed the sky once again. In minutes the sun would peek fully over the top of the horizon and they would no longer have the advantage of semidarkness. They needed to move right now. "Come on, follow me." He touched her arm lightly, then took off running across the clearing.

They ran quickly, their feet barely making a sound as

they crossed the small graveled parking area and hit the boarded ramp of the dock. They didn't stop running until they crouched down behind the pumps.

"Whew." Libby expelled a gasp as she tried to catch her breath. She sat down on the wooden dock. "Do you think anyone saw us?"

Tony shrugged. "We'll see," he said tersely, praying the store hadn't been under surveillance, praying their luck held until Cliff and his men arrived.

Libby leaned her head back against the gas pump. She was tired, tired of the whole mess. She was suddenly anxious to give the necklace to the proper people. She should be feeling euphoric—they had almost made it. But instead she felt a weary resignation she'd never known before. She looked at Tony, loving him…wishing things were different between them. She hadn't allowed her heart to listen to his denial of love the night before. But this morning his words, combined with the bittersweetness of the kiss they had shared, caused a dreaded heaviness in her heart.

She sighed, raising her face to the healing warmth of the sun as it suddenly shot over the horizon and fell brightly to earth.

She turned and peered in the direction of the grocery store as he heard the crunching of gravel beneath car tires. A black Mustang pulled up and came to a stop in front of the grocery store. "It's them, isn't it?" she whispered anxiously to Tony.

"Probably." His eyes narrowed as he stared at the car. So far, nobody had gotten out. "Just be patient." Another minute passed, then Tony hissed a curse.

Fear clutched Libby's heart as she peered around the side of the pump. Her heart plummeted to her stomach as she saw the albino and the husky, dark-haired man get out of the car. For a moment they looked around, then focused on the pumps at the end of the dock. She moaned softly as they approached the edge of the dock, both with guns in their hands. "How did they know we were here?" she whispered, unsurprised when Tony merely shrugged, his eyes black and intense.

"Mrs. Weatherby, the sun catches your blond hair like a beacon," the husky man called as he and the albino stepped onto the end of the dock. It rocked and swayed gently with their weight.

Libby gasped and placed her hands over her hair. Tony pulled his gun from his boot with one hand, and with the other hand he drew her closer to his side.

"Mr. Maxwell was most helpful in providing us with the information that you were meeting people here this morning," the dark-haired man continued. "Of course, it took considerable persuasion to get him to part with this information." Libby moaned, thinking of Jonathon Maxwell's intelligent, soft brown eyes, wondering if the lab assistant was now dead. Tears misted her vision at the thought. "You have provided us with some pleasant diversions, but this is where the game ends." The light amusement in the man's voice changed to harsh demand. "You will please come out and give us the necklace now."

"Go to hell," Tony answered, his voice filled with a deceptive laziness.

"Ah, Mr. Pandolinni, let's all be reasonable. You have no place to run, no place to hide. You have one gun, we have many. We will eventually get the necklace. You may as well cooperate with us now." He took a step forward on the dock, jerking back as Tony fired a shot, the bullet whizzing harmlessly over the man's head.

"It looks like a stalemate to me," Tony yelled. "If anyone steps another foot on the dock, I'll shoot them." Tony stalled for time. Where the hell was Cliff?

Hawk signaled and a man appeared from the woods. The new man advanced cautiously, passing where Hawk and the albino stood. Tony's muscles tightened as the man stepped up on the dock. He heard Libby's swift intake of breath as she realized they were challenging his threat.

The man advanced another two steps down the dock. Libby knew Tony was going to have to shoot him. Her sensibilities fought against her sense of survival. She didn't want him to shoot anyone, yet she knew it would make the difference between life and death for them. She closed her eyes as Tony's gun exploded. She heard the agonized cry of the man and opened her eyes to see him grabbing his leg, blood spilling over his fingertips.

With the groans of a wild, hurt animal, he pulled himself off the dock and back up the bank. Once there, two more men ran out of the woods and helped the wounded man back to the safety of the brush. Hawk signaled and another man took his place at the end of the dock.

"Son of a bitch," Tony hissed as the second man took two steps toward where he and Libby were hidden behind the gas pumps. "He's going to sacrifice his men until I'm out of bullets," Tony said, a sense of despair washing over him. How could they win against someone who would consciously allow his men to be shot like sitting ducks, killed for the sake of forcing Tony to use all his bullets? The man had no soul.

"What...what are we going to do?" Libby tried to keep the fear out of her trembling voice.

"The first thing I'm going to do is this—" He raised his gun and shot the second man, hitting him in the shoulder. As the man fell to the dock in an agony of wails and cries, Tony grabbed the bottom of his T-shirt and with a vicious yank, he tore half the bottom off.

"What...what are you doing?" she gasped, staring at him incredulously.

"Wait a minute," he muttered, pulling his cigarette lighter from his pocket. She watched silently as he took the material and stuffed it into the nozzle of the gas pump.

He turned and looked at her, his eyes so black it was impossible to discern the pupil from the iris. "When I tell you to jump, I want you to run and jump off the dock and swim like hell for the opposite shore."

"No." She stared at him with widened eyes. "What are you going to do?"

"I'm going to blow this dock to kingdom come," he said tersely. "If you can get to the other shore, you should be safe there until Cliff gets here."

"But...but what about you?" She stared at him painfully. "Tony, isn't there some other way?"

He reached out and touched her face softly. "Libby, I've got three bullets left, and those guys are just going to send out three more men for me to shoot, then they'll be down here for us. This is our only chance. The necklace is what's important. You've got to swim for your life."

"But, Tony, I don't want to leave you...." She heard a slight edge of hysteria in her own voice.

"Libby, when I say jump, damn it, you jump and you swim," he exploded angrily, turning his attention to the men on the shore. They had managed to remove the second injured man from the edge of the dock.

"Mr. Pandolinni, must we continue to waste more of my men before you come to your senses and surrender?'' Hawk yelled. ''I must admit, I am losing patience.''

''Get ready,'' Tony said to Libby, lighting the edge of the material that hung out of the gas nozzle. As the material began to flame, Tony stood up and fired the last of his bullets. ''Now,'' he yelled.

In one quick movement, Libby ran and dove off the end of the dock, the shock of the icy-cold lake water stealing her breath away. She swam for some distance beneath the water, then broke the surface with a gasp for breath. Immediately, there was a loud explosion behind her. A wave of heat hit her as scattering debris plopped in the water around her. In horror she turned around to look at the dock. The place where she and Tony had been hiding was in flames. There was no sign of the two gas pumps, and no sign of Tony.

''Tony?'' The name was a mere whisper on her lips as she tread water and stared at the place where he had been when she had last seen him. Had he jumped in time? Had he managed to get away before the explosion?

She stared at the dark water between her and the dock, waiting breathlessly for his dark head to pop up out of the water, watching anxiously for some sign that he had made it and was alive. Seconds passed...minutes...too long for anyone to hold their breath beneath the surface of the water.

''Tony.'' This time his name tore from her throat as a wave of agony washed over her. He couldn't be gone. He couldn't be. A sob caught in her throat. Still, there was no sign of him anywhere. She sobbed again and turned around. The opposite shore looked distant, too far for her to reach. ''But you have to,'' she gasped aloud, knowing that if she didn't make it to the other shore and wait for Cliff and the proper authorities, then all of this had been for nothing.

She squeezed her eyes tightly closed for a moment, fighting against the desire just to give up and sink to the bottom of the lake. She touched the necklace that hung heavily around her neck, then began to swim for the opposite shoreline.

She'd gone only a few yards when one of her legs was grasped in a viselike grip. As she screamed, her head plunged beneath the surface of the water. She kicked out and surfaced, coughing and choking on the mouthful of water she'd swallowed. She shoved her hair off her face and opened her eyes to find herself staring into the cold, colorless eyes of the albino.

"You're mine, bitch," he snarled, reaching out to grab her once again.

She screamed again, hysterically kicking away from him, her arms and legs flailing frantically in her effort to escape his grasp. She managed two strokes, hissing in pain as her hair was grabbed from behind and she was once again plunged beneath the water.

She struggled, using her fingernails to gouge and scratch, her feet to kick. She needed air. Her lungs burned painfully and the need to gasp was overwhelming. She kicked again, grunting as her foot found his groin and caused him to loosen his grasp on her hair. It was all she needed. She twisted out of his grasp and broke the surface of the water, gasping deeply, taking in painful gulps of air.

She was aware of the sound of a boat. She also heard a sound like an enraged bull behind her, and before she had a chance to react, she was dragged downward yet again. This time, her struggles were slower, less frantic as exhaustion overtook her. Tony was dead, and she was tired...so tired. She could see tiny bubbles escaping her lips and floating upward to the surface, but she felt no panic. Instead, she quit struggling altogether. A curious sense of well-being swept over her. *It's not so bad,* she thought with a sense of surprise. *It's not so bad to drown.*

Suddenly the arms that had been holding her down in the water were gone, and she rose easily to the top of the water. She rolled over on her back and it was then that the pain struck her. She choked and gagged, her lungs burning as fresh air flowed into her lungs.

She was vaguely aware of a pair of strong arms reaching beneath her and lifting her up into a boat. So, they had won after all, she thought tiredly. They had managed to kill Tony and now they would take the necklace from her and then they would kill her.

As a warm blanket was placed around her shivering body, she frowned in confusion. Why were they being so nice to her? Why give a blanket to a woman they were going to kill? She opened her eyes and found herself looking into the face of a clean-cut, blond-haired man. "Cliff?" she croaked hopefully.

He nodded and gave her a reassuring grin. "Don't worry, you're safe now."

"Tony..." Tears spurted to her eyes as she tried to find the words to tell Cliff that his friend was dead, that Tony had made the ultimate sacrifice for the safety of his country.

Cliff's grin widened. "Yeah, he was really something else, wasn't he? I didn't even know Pandolinni could swim. But he cut through the water like a torpedo when he saw that fellow going after you."

"But...I thought..." Libby stared at Cliff in shock, his words causing a pleasurable tingle to begin flowing through her body. Tony was alive…he was alive! "Where is he?"

Cliff pointed to the shore near the grocery store. The area was crawling with uniformed officers, and it was easy to see that Cliff had the situation completely under control. Among the men handcuffed and in custody, Libby recognized the burly, dark-haired man and the albino. She sobbed with pleasure as she saw Tony standing at the edge of the lake, his gaze directed on her as the small motorboat carried her to the shore.

"Tony!" Before the boat even docked, she jumped out and into his arms.

For a moment they stood, as if all alone in the world, holding each other close. "Oh, God, Tony…I thought— I didn't see you and I…"

"Shh." Tony pulled her closer into his arms and stroked her hair. "And when I saw that madman swimming after you…I thought—" His voice broke off as he saw Cliff approaching them. "I told you there was a beautiful blonde," he told him with a grin, releasing his hold on Libby.

"Yeah, although you neglected to mention that you had most of the members of the New Republic of Man itching to kill you." Cliff grinned good-naturedly at Tony. "It's a good thing I know your tendency to underestimate the danger you're in. I brought a small army with me to help you out of this sticky situation." He turned at the approach of two other men. "Tony…these are two friends of mine. I don't think names are really important."

"We would like to have the necklace," one of the men said softly, his blank gaze on Libby and the jewelry around her neck.

She looked at Tony for confirmation. When he nodded

his assent, she slowly unfastened the necklace from around her neck and handed it to the tall, distinguished man who'd requested it. "It's on the back," she explained.

He took it gingerly, eyeing the back of the locket with interest. "Hopefully the water didn't hurt it," he said, carefully removing the dark chip and holding it in the palm of his hand.

For the first time, Libby noticed the other man had a small laptop computer opened and readied. She watched curiously as he bent over it now, calling up the formula on the screen.

"Is this some kind of a joke?" One of the men glared first at Libby, then at Tony.

"What do you mean?" Tony asked, looking bewildered.

"This formula won't work."

"Did the water ruin the chip?" Libby asked curiously.

"No, the chip is fine. But the formula is bogus."

Tony's frown deepened as Libby returned his look of bewilderment. "I don't understand!" she exclaimed. "What's wrong with it?"

"It would be impossible to create this particular formula. Our present technology simply isn't capable. It's based on the theory of a disbursement of human cells, a feat science has yet to accomplish." He shut off the computer and shook his head. "It's not worth the cost of the chip."

Libby stared at him in horror. All the danger, all the life-threatening situations they had been in...and it had all been for a formula that wouldn't, couldn't work.

Tony sighed in wonderment. "Jasper Higgens apparently went off the deep end when his wife died. I wonder if he really believed it would work.'' He shook his head slowly.

The tall man sighed and held out the necklace to Libby. ''This is yours. The man who owned it is dead and legally it belongs to you.''

Libby hesitated, then took the necklace.

''It will make a nice memento for you—sort of a reminder of the time you were involved in national intrigue,'' Tony said.

She looked up at him, controlling the shiver as she sensed his withdrawal from her. ''Yes, it will make a nice memento,'' she echoed vaguely. It was over. Whatever they had shared was gone now.

''Well, let's get out of here. We have some debriefing to put you all through,'' the tall man explained. He turned and yelled orders to his men concerning the prisoners they had arrested, then turned back to Tony and Libby. ''Ma'am, I'll be glad to give you a ride back to Kansas City. I'll debrief you on the way and you can get back to your normal life.'' He eyed Tony. ''Mr. Pandolinni, I'll be glad to give you a ride, also.''

''No, that's all right. I have my own car. Cliff can ride back with me and he'll debrief me.'' Tony's gaze refused to meet Libby's eyes.

''Well, let's hit the road,'' the tall man instructed, courteously leading Libby toward his car. She slid into the passenger seat, turning to look back to where Cliff and Tony stood.

Her gaze met Tony's, and the dark, shuttered look in his eyes told her it was over. Not only the danger, and the intrigue, but the love, as well.

For a moment she couldn't breathe and it was like being underwater all over again. She wanted to jump out of the car, run back to where he stood and throw her arms around him, hold him until he admitted that he loved her…that he couldn't live without her. But she couldn't do that. She couldn't fight his demons for him. He would have to do that for himself.

She broke the gaze, unable to withstand it any longer. Mechanically, she fastened her seat belt. As the car pulled away from Walker's Grocery, she looked back once again, needing one last, lingering look at the man she loved, the man she knew she would never see again.

Chapter 15

Libby coughed and choked as dust flew around the shop as she methodically ran a feather duster over the wooden shelf that held a variety of knickknacks. In the past three weeks she had thrown herself into a marathon cleaning of the pawnshop. She had scrubbed the large picture windows until they sparkled and gleamed. Each and every item the shop held had been dusted and waxed, wiped and polished. She'd rearranged shelves, scrubbed the floor, set up new displays…all in an effort to stay busy and exhausted. She'd thought that if she stayed busy enough, if she remained exhausted enough, she would forget Tony Pandolinni. But it didn't work.

She sat back on her haunches, the feather duster falling idle in her hands, thinking back over the past three weeks.

Sam, the man who had driven her back to Kansas City from the Ozarks, had been very kind. Her debriefing had existed of her simply being told not to mention to anyone any of the events that had transpired concerning the New Republic of Man group, and the formula. She was more than ready to forget the fear, the terror she'd experienced during those few days.

What she couldn't forget was Tony.

She wondered if the day would ever come when a full twenty-four hours would pass and she wouldn't think of him, wouldn't remember the splendor of lying in his arms. Even now, after three weeks, when she closed her eyes, she could still remember the heady scent of his skin, the texture of his flesh beneath her fingertips, the sensation of completeness when he surged inside her. God, if only her memory bank could be emptied like the till of her cash register. If only each memory of him could be erased forever from her mind.

At least one good thing had transpired in the past three weeks. Bill had found a new love. He'd brought her into the pawnshop the day before, a shy little redhead named Jenny. She'd looked at Bill with adoring eyes, hanging on his every word as if he spoke only the most profound statements. She was just the kind of woman Bill needed, and Libby was happy for her ex-husband...and happy for herself because she knew there would be no more private investigators shadowing her movements. Her life was her own...and she wished she could share it with Tony.

"Face the fact, Libby old girl," she now said softly, moving the feather duster once again across the emptied shelf. "It's done...over." Time to put thoughts of Tony Pandolinni out of her head, time to shut him out of her heart.

She set the feather duster down and began arranging the figurines and brass items on the newly dusted space. She sighed as the small bell above the door tinkled, announcing that somebody had entered the shop. She glanced at her wristwatch and frowned. Why did people always bring in a load of junk to pawn just before closing time?

"I'll be with you in a second," she yelled, placing a brass elephant on the shelf, then standing and brushing off the seat of her pants. She looked up, and shock rippled through her as she saw Tony standing just inside the doorway.

Neither of them spoke a word. For a long moment, Libby simply stood and looked at him, drinking in his features as shock rendered her speechless.

He wore a uniform—the blue shirt and slacks of the police department. His hair was slightly unruly, as if he'd run his hands through it many times in the past few hours. His face looked thinner, more haggard than she remembered. Yet it was his eyes that captured and held her gaze. They were dark orbs glittering with an emotion she couldn't quite define.

"Hi," he said simply.

"Hello," she responded, trying to settle her suddenly jumbled thoughts, needing to hang on to her heart, which thudded erratically in her chest. The implication of his uniform suddenly penetrated her mind. "You rejoined the police force," she said.

He nodded. "Last week. You were right when you told me I should do it. It's who I am. I was crazy to think I wanted to be a P.I."

"So…uh…what brings you to this part of town?" she asked, trying to keep her tone light and neutral. She didn't want to jump to conclusions. She wouldn't be able to stand it if she was disappointed again.

He walked around the shop, picking up first one item, then another, obviously discomforted. "I just wondered if you'd gotten everything back in order here. Did you have any problems filing your insurance claim?''

For a moment she stared at him, wondering if the sole reason for his visit was a professional one. Did he not realize that the mere sight of him tore her heart inside out?

"No...no problems," she replied. "But thank you for the courtesy of stopping by." She raised her chin a fraction of an inch, refusing to give in to the tears that pressed hotly against the back of her eyelids. She refused to let him see that he was ripping her apart inside.

"Well, I guess your life has calmed down considerably in the past couple of weeks?" He shifted from foot to foot, his gaze not quite meeting hers.

"It's amazing how getting out of the middle of a national security crisis can simplify your life," she retorted, aware that her voice was slightly sarcastic.

She was beginning to get angry. His very presence here in her shop was starting to make her mad as hell. How dare he barge back into her life when he obviously didn't want to do anything but touch base with her as some sort of a damned professional courtesy?

"Now, if you'll excuse me...I was just getting ready to close up for the night." She walked over to the window and flipped the Closed sign, opened the door, then looked at him expectantly.

"Well...uh, I don't want to keep you...." He started for the door, pausing a moment with his hand on the doorknob. He looked at her as if he wanted to say something more, then quickly disappeared out the door.

Libby's breath whooshed out of her, a trembling sigh of heartbreak. On wooden legs, she pushed the door closed and started to lock the dead bolt. She jumped as

Tony suddenly reappeared at the door. He motioned for her to unlock it.

"Did you forget something?" she asked, opening the door and letting him back in.

"Yes, I did." Without warning, he grabbed her to him, his lips claiming hers in a kiss that instantly stole her breath away.

For just a single moment, she fought him, not wanting to fall into the magic of his kiss, the wonder of being in his arms so easily. She wanted to sustain her anger, she needed to deny her love, but with a slight groan of acquiescence, she kissed him back with all the passion, all the desire and all the love that was in her heart.

When he finally pulled his mouth from hers, he placed his hands on either side of her face and smiled. "Ah, Libby, what have you done to me? I've tried to stay away from you—I've tried to convince myself that we're far better off apart. Every morning I wake up and promise myself I won't think about you. I won't remember holding you in my arms. Every day I promise myself, today I won't love her. Today I won't want her."

"Tony Pandolinni, you have some nerve, coming in here and kissing me, sweet-talking me after three weeks of being absent from my life," Libby exclaimed, unwilling to let him off the hook so easily. She pushed her way out of his arms and glared at him.

He threw back his head and laughed, obviously delighted with her ire. "Ah, Libby, whatever made me worry that you would be the kind of woman who'd get lost in the shadows? I keep pushing you back into the shadows of my mind, but you refuse to stay there." He leaned forward and with the tips of his fingers swept an errant strand of her hair away from her cheek. "I have been so afraid for so long of being like my father. I quit my job on the force so that wouldn't happen. I've kept myself isolated and alone so I wouldn't ruin somebody else's life like he destroyed my mother's.''

"But you aren't your father," she reminded him softly, knowing Tony could never be cold, unemotional.

"No," he agreed. "I'm not my father, and I don't think there's anything or anyone on this earth that could make you a shadow woman. You'll never fade away—you're too strong for that." He took her back into his arms, his body pressing intimately against hers. "I love you, Libby. If you're willing to take a chance on a stubborn cop who works long hours for too little pay, I'm willing to take a chance on an outspoken, stubborn pawnshop owner. Marry me... I need you beside me."

She threw her arms around his neck, joy causing tears to spring to her eyes. "I thought you were going to stay a fool forever," she breathed, pulling his head down so their lips could meet in a kiss of infinite tenderness.

"I may be slow, but nobody can tell me I'm a complete fool," he murmured against her lips. "After facing the likes of an albino psychopath and a group of subversives, do you think you're woman enough to put up with me?"

She smiled up at him, her heart filled with a kind of love she'd never experienced before. It consumed her, overwhelmed her, and she knew it would sustain her forever. "Yes, Tony." She placed her hand on the side of his face, loving the look in his eyes, loving everything about him. "Didn't I tell you that you were one of the good guys?"

"Yeah, I guess it just took a while for me to realize that," he replied softly.

Libby smiled at him. "I intend to spend every day of

the rest of my life reminding you of just how good you are.''

He smiled and his eyes lit up with a fire that made a glow deep inside her. ''How about we start right now in your back room?'' he asked, nuzzling her neck in a way that made it impossible for her to think. And as he swept her up into his arms and headed for the back room, she knew there would be moments in her marriage to Tony when she would worry about his safety. There would be times they wouldn't agree. But he would allow her to be herself—he loved her for the outspoken, stubborn fool that she was. They hadn't found a formula that would save the world, but they had found the formula for love, and in the end, that was all that really mattered.

* * * * *

HEROES
AGAINST ALL ODDS

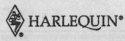

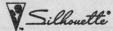

Please address questions and book requests to: Harlequin Reader Service U.S.: 3010 Walden Ave.,
P.O. Box 1325, Buffalo, NY 14269 CAN.: P.O. Box 609, Fort Erie, Ont. L2A 5X3   PAHGEN

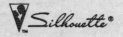

FOUR UNIQUE SERIES
FOR EVERY WOMAN YOU ARE...

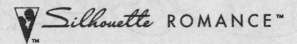 **Silhouette ROMANCE™**

These entertaining, tender and involving love stories
celebrate the spirit of pure romance.

Desire.

Desire features strong heroes and spirited heroines
who come together in a highly passionate,
emotionally powerful and always provocative read.

Silhouette® SPECIAL EDITION®

For every woman who dreams of life, love and family,
these are the romances in which she makes
her dreams come true.

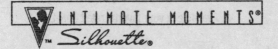 **INTIMATE MOMENTS®** **Silhouette®**

Dive into the pages of Intimate Moments and experience
adventure and excitement in these complex
and dramatic romances.

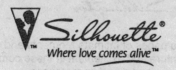

Celebrate Silhouette's 20th Anniversary

With beloved authors, exciting new miniseries and special keepsake collections, **plus** the chance to enter our 20th anniversary contest, in which one lucky reader wins the trip of a lifetime!

Take a look at who's celebrating with us:

DIANA PALMER

April 2000: SOLDIERS OF FORTUNE
May 2000 in Silhouette Romance: *Mercenary's Woman*

NORA ROBERTS

May 2000: IRISH HEARTS, the 2-in-1 keepsake collection
June 2000 in Special Edition: *Irish Rebel*

LINDA HOWARD

July 2000: MacKENZIE'S MISSION
August 2000 in Intimate Moments: *A Game of Chance*

ANNETTE BROADRICK

October 2000: a special keepsake collection, plus a brand-new title in
November 2000 in Desire

Available at your favorite retail outlet.

Where love comes alive™

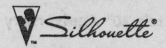